It was the war cry that almost did Chance in. It seemed to explode out of nowhere, starting as a guttural growl and ending in a series of high-pitched yips more like that of a frightened coyote than a human being. Chance froze, waiting for the Apache to lean over the wall and take another shot.

Instead, the Apache charged down the steep path, his moccasined feet surefooted and silent on the treacherous rock. He waved the rifle high overhead and let out another war cry.

Chance was stunned into immobility. The Indian reached the first cutback and changed course with ease. The next leg of the path was narrower, and the Apache stumbled, losing his balance for a long moment. He seemed to hang motionless, then reached out with one hand, managed to right himself, and plunged on. He never even slowed down after the momentary break in his stride.

Then, as if he had just awakened, the Indian looked at him. He smiled a strange smile and raised his weapon. Chance tried to crawl into the stone, but he couldn't move.

By Bill Dugan

DUEL ON THE MESA
TEXAS DRIVE
GUN PLAY AT CROSS CREEK
BRADY'S LAW
DEATH SONG
MADIGAN'S LUCK

War Chiefs

GERONIMO
CHIEF JOSEPH
CRAZY HORSE
QUANAH PARKER
SITTING BULL

ATTENTION: ORGANIZATIONS AND CORPORATIONS
Most HarperTorch paperbacks are available at special quantity discounts for bulk purchases for sales promotions, premiums, or fund-raising. For information, please call or write:

Special Markets Department, HarperCollins Publishers, Inc.,
10 East 53rd Street, New York, N.Y. 10022–5299.
Telephone: (212) 207–7528. Fax: (212) 207-7222.

BILL DUGAN

Duel on the Mesa

HarperTorch
An Imprint of HarperCollinsPublishers

This is a work of fiction. Names, characters, places, and incidents are products of the author's imagination or are used fictitiously and are not to be construed as real. Any resemblance to actual events, locales, organizations, or persons, living or dead, is entirely coincidental.

HARPERTORCH
An Imprint of HarperCollins*Publishers*
10 East 53rd Street
New York, New York 10022-5299

Copyright © 1990 by Charlie McDade
ISBN: 0-06-100033-7

All rights reserved. No part of this book may be used or reproduced in any manner whatsoever without written permission, except in the case of brief quotations embodied in critical articles and reviews. For information address HarperTorch, an Imprint of HarperCollins Publishers.

First HarperTorch paperback printing: April 2003
First HarperCollins paperback printing: June 1990

HarperCollins ®, HarperTorch™, and ♥ ™ are trademarks of HarperCollins Publishers Inc.

Printed in the United States of America

Visit HarperTorch on the World Wide Web at www.harpercollins.com

10 9 8 7 6 5 4 3

If you purchased this book without a cover, you should be aware that this book is stolen property. It was reported as "unsold and destroyed" to the publisher, and neither the author nor the publisher has received any payment for this "stripped book."

1

DALTON CHANCE HEARD the first shot like a distant echo. He knew right away what it was. It was a rifle, and it was high above him. He glanced up at the rim rock, then dug his spurs into his mount and charged straight for the vertical wall two hundred yards away. A second shot cracked from the same place, and this time the bullet didn't miss by much. He heard it whistle just past his right ear and a little high.

The shooter was still out of sight, but Chance had no doubt in his mind that he was the target. As his horse closed on the rocky rubble at the foot of the cliff, he slowed a bit, then angled to the left. Eighty yards down the wall, he reined in, leaving the saddle on the fly, and jerking his carbine out of its boot in the same fluid motion.

Racing for a cantilevered slab of red rock,

braced off the ground by a pair of roundish boulders, he nearly slipped and fell. As it was, he had to catch himself to avoid crashing into the rocks. The impact sent a stab of pain up his left arm, and his wrist started to throb. Ignoring the pain, he scrambled under the overhanging slab and strained his ears.

The shooter no longer had a clear line of sight. The wall towering above him was more than two hundred feet, straight up. Anyone on the rim would have to lean out and over just to see where Chance lay hidden. While he listened, he racked his brain for a clue as to who might want to kill him and why. He drew a blank on both counts.

When the pain in his wrist started to subside, he flexed it once or twice. It hurt like hell, but nothing seemed to be broken. Already, the flesh was swollen so badly that he had to unbutton his sleeve and roll it up a couple of turns. Probably sprained, he thought, pressing the swollen area with the fingers of his right hand.

Pain or not, he couldn't stay where he was. If the shooter was serious, he'd make a move soon, if he hadn't already. Chance wriggled back further under the slab and looked up at the wall towering above him. Its ragged edge was unbroken by anything but outcroppings of rock and a few stray plants, mostly cactus and a couple of tiny shrubs, barely clinging to the inhospitable rock.

If anyone was still up there, he was staying back from the rim. Chance shook his head, as if it was a sign to himself that he had made a decision. He used his right arm to haul himself back toward the front of the rock, dragging his Winchester in his injured hand. Checking the sun, he realized it was pointless to wait for dark. He had nearly three hours till sundown. By then, whoever tried to kill him would be down on the valley floor or long gone.

Chance wasn't a belligerent man, but this wasn't something he could just walk away from. It crossed his mind that it might be Apaches, but that didn't much matter. Apache bullets were no more or less deadly than those of a half-dozen other candidates. It could have been Mexican bandits from south of the border.

It could have been a white man, too, a bandit or even somebody he'd offended without realizing it. Probably not, but you never knew. People had short fuses. They took offense where none was intended. And in this brutal, barren wasteland, it sometimes seemed easier to reach for a gun than not.

Chance himself had five years of cavalry service behind him. It would have been less, but the enlistment term was five, and five was what he had to serve, even though he decided after six months he'd made the wrong decision. But that's the kind of man he was, the kind of man who followed through. If he gave his word, he kept it. If he made a commitment, he delivered, even if he had made a mistake.

He'd worked his way up to sergeant, and that was as high as he could go. That was as high as he wanted to go, anyway. He didn't understand why any man would devote his life to giving orders to other men. A man should take care of himself and his own family. Anything else was arrogance.

The thought of his family galvanized him. He had to get the hell out of here, and he had to do it soon.

He knew the terrain as well as any white man. If the shooter was an Apache, then he could be in way over his head. But he didn't flinch.

Chance hauled himself out and scrambled up on top of the slab of stone. He stared up at the rimrock, looking for some hint of where the shooter's nest could be. He knew the top of the mesa, right up to the edge of the wall, was covered with huge boulders. A man could hide up there for a week, if he wanted to. And if he didn't have a man as determined as Dalton Chance on his tail.

But if it were an Apache, even that determination wouldn't matter. They were almost ungodly, the way they could melt through rock and disappear, almost without leaving a trace. Chance had seen the Sioux, even been at the Rosebud with

Crook, and that was bad enough. But the Apache were something altogether different. It was the difference between gold and pyrite. Maybe even greater.

But it was all moot at the moment. He had to get on top, and knew of only one way up. Moving in close to the wall, Chance picked his way through the jumbled rock, stopping every fifty or sixty yards to look back toward the lip of stone overhead. It would be just his luck to run into the shooter on the way up. The trail, a path really, was narrow, and the footing treacherous. He'd only been up there once, and that on a dare. It was a dumb thing to have done, but he was young and foolish. And it made him ten dollars. This time, though, the stakes were a lot higher.

At the blunt end of the mesa, he found two horses, one saddled and one just wearing a bridle, a fresh mount. Obviously, the rider planned either on traveling a long distance, was in a hurry, or both.

And it was an Apache's pony. There was no doubt about that. The light saddle was a dead giveaway. Chance cursed under his breath. Crouching behind a large rock, he looked up toward the top of the mesa. Two hundred feet straight up, and nearly five times that on the narrow path. There wasn't half enough cover, and he thought about waiting right where he was. The Apache would have to come down sooner or later. But what if he was wrong? If there was another way down, he'd have to face the Indian in the dark on his home ground.

It would be easier to put a bullet through his own head, and probably less painful.

Counting to himself, he got to ten three different times, and each time he stopped after the first step. He almost grinned. He felt silly, like he was a kid trying to sneak home after curfew, knowing he would get caught, but not knowing what else to do.

On the fourth count, he forced himself to move, starting up quickly, and slowing only after he reached the first cutback. The path zig-zagged at a steep angle, switching back on itself with every thirty or forty vertical feet. He was just entering the next leg when a rock skidded above him, clattered down the path, skipping past him and bouncing out in a high arc. Chance watched the rock all the way out of sight. He heard it hit before he dared to look up again.

He couldn't see anyone, but the chances it was just a stray falling rock seemed to him rather slim. He held his breath and levered a shell into the chamber of the Winchester, trying to muffle the click with his hands as best he could.

He thought for a second about backing down the path, but it wasn't really a serious consideration.

Somebody had tried to kill him, and he'd be damned if he'd run. Taking a deep breath, he started into the next leg of the path, covering the whole distance to the next switchback before he stopped to look up again. He kept resisting the temptation to watch the rim, but a false step now would kill him as surely as any bullet. Better to worry about the Apache when, and if, he managed to make it to the top.

The third leg was narrower than the first two, and Chance almost had to walk on the edges of his bootsoles to keep from slipping off the rock and crashing down into the boulders far below him. Still no sign of the Indian. He leaned in against the wall, his Winchester parallel to the rock face and all but useless. The rest of the path was better, but he still had sixty or seventy feet before he reached more secure footing.

Another rock skipped past him. The rifle cracked again. The report startled him, and he almost lost his footing.

But it was the war cry that almost did him in. It seemed to explode out of nowhere, starting as a guttural growl and ending in a series of high-pitched yips more like that of a frightened coyote than a human being. Chance froze, waiting for the Apache to lean over the wall and take another shot.

Instead, the Indian charged over the rimrock and hit the path at a full gallop. Like a madman, he charged down the steep path, his moccasined feet surefooted and silent on the treacherous rock. The Apache fired his rifle again, but not at Chance. Instead, he waved the rifle high overhead and let out another war cry.

Chance was stunned into immobility. The Indian reached the first cutback and changed course with ease, as graceful as the ballet dancer Chance had seen in St. Louis. That had amazed him, and it was on a flat stage. This was grace in its superhuman form. Chance wanted to raise his own rifle, but he knew he would fall if he tried.

The Apache seemed unaware of him, which hardly seemed possible. After all, he thought, the bastard was shooting at me. The next leg of the path was narrower, and the Apache stumbled, losing his balance for a long moment. He seemed to hang motionless, then reached out with one hand, managed to right himself, and plunged on. He never even slowed down after the momentary break in his stride.

Then, as if he had just awakened, the Indian looked at him. He smiled a strange smile and raised his weapon. Chance tried to crawl into the stone, but he couldn't move. He watched as the Apache's rifle wavered for a second, then, his eyes on Chance, he missed a step.

The Apache teetered precariously and the gun barrel swept up as its owner's hands pinwheeled in the air. Then the rifle slipped out of his grasp and it turned once in the air. Weighed down by the heavy stock, it fell butt first, glanced off the stone wall, and narrowly missed Chance as it plummeted past.

The Indian came next, feet first. His head slammed back into the rock, his hands clawing at the stone beside his hips as he tried to slow his fall enough to arrest it at the next level of the path. By that time, he was moving too fast for anything to slow him down. He howled again, and reached out for Chance with desperate, claw-like hands as he went by, whether to save his own life or to drag Chance with him. Chance didn't know.

For one crazy second, he thought about trying to grab the Apache, but he knew the impact would break his own hold and carry him onto the jagged rocks below.

The Indian's rifle went off when it hit. A moment later, the dull thud of flesh on stone signalled the end of the Apache's descent. It got very quiet.

A handful of loose rocks showered down, landing with barely audible cracks, skittered to a standstill, and the quiet returned. Chance was aware of his ragged breathing. His throat felt raw, as if it had been scraped with sandpaper. His mouth was dry, his tongue like a piece of leather, and he couldn't stand the taste. He swallowed hard, trying to control his breathing and regain his composure.

When he felt in control again, he started back down the path, his steps small and tentative. Every time he placed a boot, he felt sure he was going to lose his foothold. With painful slowness, he worked his way back to the wider section of the path, stopped to take a few deep breaths, then moved the rest of the way down. He spotted the Apache right away. The Indian had landed on a large boulder and now lay draped over it, curled out of shape like a dead fish.

Chance scrambled up onto the boulder and knelt beside the Indian. There was surprisingly little blood. But Chance could tell by the awkward posture that the Apache had broken his back, probably in more than once place. A trickle of blood ran from one corner of the Apache's mouth, more from both ears.

Over the smell of death was a faint hint of something else, not altogether unpleasant. It took Chance a moment to place it, and when he did, he understood what had happened.

It was alcohol. Selling whiskey to the Indians was illegal. Anyone in Cotton Springs knew that. Hell, anyone in Arizona knew that. They weren't that far from the reservation at San Carlos, and most people in the area had had more than their share of trouble with the Apaches.

Chance looked up at the sun, judged he had enough time to bury the Indian before heading back. He'd have to ride into Cotton Springs in the morning and tell Tom Walker about it. Whether Sheriff Walker could do anything about it was unlikely.

But somebody better do something. If the Apaches were getting their hands on a regular supply of whiskey, nobody was safe.

2

CHANCE WAS SHAKING. He felt something in his stomach that wanted to come up, and he tried to fight it off. Walking back to his horse, he snatched at his canteen, took a mouthful of spit-warm water and swirled it around, then swallowed. He hoped it would settle his stomach.

It didn't.

What the hell was he going to do? He didn't want to leave the Apache's corpse lying there for the buzzards and the coyotes to pick over, but what if the Indian had companions? Suppose they saw him with the body draped over the Indian's saddle? One drunken Indian was one thing, but a pack of Apaches would be a horse of a different color.

He walked back to the body, half hoping it wouldn't be there.

It was.

Chance looked at the sky, judging the daylight. There wasn't much left, but he couldn't just leave. But he sure as hell wasn't going to break a sweat digging a hole under this scalding sun. Not if he didn't have to, anyway. Cursing under his breath, he looked around for a flat spot to lay the corpse. Against the base of the mesa wall, he found a niche big enough to hold the dead man. It would have to do.

Shaking his head, he trudged back to the dead Apache, dragging his feet and kicking at stray rocks like a kid who doesn't want to go to school. Bugs were already beginning to move in. Flies snarled angrily at him as he reached for an arm, and the trickle of blood running down over the rocks had already brought a few ants. The word would get out and they'd be all over the place in a few minutes.

Nothing like a dead body, Chance thought, to prove there's life in the goddamned desert. He tugged on the arm, but the body didn't want to move. Grabbing it with both hands, he hauled the body partway off the rock, then shrugged. There was no point in making it any harder than it had to be. He moved in close, careful to avoid getting the blood on his clothes, and picked the corpse up.

The Apache was surprisingly heavy. Short and stocky, like most of his tribe, he must have been all muscle and bone. It seemed like he weighed a ton.

Staggering back away from the big rock, he almost lost his balance. The body smelled from voided bowels and bladder, and the buckskin leggings were sticky. Chance didn't even want to know with what. When he regained his balance, he groaned under the weight of the dead buck, but managed to cover the fifty or sixty feet to the small crevice.

Then he turned to the rocks. They had to be small enough for him to move but heavy enough to make a scavenger think twice. It looked like every rock in creation lay there on the floor of the canyon, and he had no trouble building a cairn. Picking rocks pretty much of the same size and shape, he was able to fashion a neat, effective wall.

When he was done, his shirt was soaked through, and he was winded. His hands were ripped and bloody from the sharp edges of the stones, and he stank. But he had done the right thing. Or so he told himself.

That left only the matter of the brave's horses and possessions. He'd thought about burying the latter with the body, but the Apaches had precious little as it was. It didn't make sense to bury something the man's family, if he had one, could use, if they ever got it back. Chance took the pair of horses, dragged them grudgingly to the graveside and piled the Apache's belongings next to the neat pile of stones. Then he cut the horses lose, shouted at them and gave one a swat on the rump. They moved off a way, not in any hurry, then stood, as if watching him.

Chance shook his head. He'd done as much as he could. Now all he had to do was make it back to the ranch before sundown, no small order.

He took another pull on his canteen before mounting up. Moving past the grave, his horse shied a little, probably scenting the corpse. He tipped his hat and moved on.

Chance felt a little embarrassed. Most of the ranchers in these parts would have left the Apache where he fell, but Chance wasn't made that way. A man was a man, Apache or no. He didn't know their customs, but he did what he'd want somebody to do for him. Not that he ever expected to get roaring drunk and fall the hell off a mesa.

But you never know what might happen to you. For all he knew, he might not make it home himself. It gave him some comfort thinking maybe somebody would look out for his mortal coil the way he'd done for the Apache.

Fat chance. He almost smiled at the thought. Arizona was a hard place to make a living, and an even harder one to make a life. The Apaches were one of the main reasons, but they had some reason to gripe. Ripped off their land, which they didn't understand, and forced to live within the confines of the San Carlos Reservation, which they didn't understand either, they were resentful, and they had a right to be. They didn't understand the white man's ways, and that wasn't so surprising, because there were times when Chance didn't understand them either. But it was the land that was the main problem. To the Apache, land wasn't something you owned, it was where you were, something you were part of, nothing more and nothing less.

They had a reputation for brutality, and Chance knew all the bloody details. He'd seen their handiwork twice himself. He hoped to God he never saw it again. Fact was, what he'd seen made him wonder if there was a God at all. And if there was, he sure as hell didn't have a hand in shaping the Apache. Not that there was any suitable clay for His purpose in Arizona.

He remembered old man Sigafoos, Wilhelm it was, the poor dumb bastard. Thought he could make a stand when any man with half a brain was running for Fort Bowie. Sigafoos thought they were all crazy. "You don't leaf your schtuff for nobody to schteal, dummkopf," he'd said. "Them safages burn mein house, I leaf it mit nobody vatching."

But Sigafoos was wrong. The Apaches didn't burn the house. Oh, they built a fire alright, a big one. Right between his legs. When they found him two days later, Wilhelm looked like leftover barbecue. It was the face that would stay with Chance, though. The skin was all blistered, the chin and nose crisp and black, the rest bright red. And the eyes were already gone, just slimy holes left where the bugs got to them.

That was the Apache for you, Chance thought. But they weren't entirely in the wrong. He just hoped like hell he didn't have to explain his relatively benign view to a handful of the dead buck's compadres.

It was almost sundown, and Chance felt like somebody was watching him. He knew it was probably just nerves. But he did what anybody with any sense does when he feels like that. He acts like it's true and runs like hell. He whipped the hell out of the horse until his arm was tired. Then he used his spurs. He was tired and he was thirsty and he wasn't about to stop for anything short of a cavalry detachment.

Down the back of his spine, it felt like every nerve was frozen. He was shivering, and he couldn't stop. And he didn't give a damn. Right now, all he wanted to do was ride into his own yard and see Jenny on the front porch, wringing her hands in her apron that way she did, chewing at her lower lip. He always teased her about that, told her she'd give herself buck teeth. But tonight, he was chewing on his own lip.

After five miles of flat out riding, he slowed his horse to a walk. He was breathing hard, the horse even harder. Trying to sort it out in his own mind, he found himself confused by what had happened. The Apache wanted to kill him, sure enough, but why?

There was no answer except the whiskey, unless he wanted to fall back on the one answer he would never accept easily—that Indians were like that. You couldn't trust them, and given the chance, the Indian would turn on you every time. That was too simplistic, and he'd seen too many instances that proved the contrary.

Riding with Crook, he had learned, as his commanding officer had, to trust the red man. Forthrightness and honor were universals, Crook had insisted. And he had been proven right time and time again.

Over his five years in the army, he had seen it over and over. If you dug deep enough, there was an answer for every apparent treachery. Most had greed at the bottom, white man's greed, not Indian greed. There was always an excuse—gold in the Black Hills, the railroad has to have a right of way, we need fur for ladies' hats. And always, the excuse ignored the Indian reality—the Black Hills were sacred to the Sioux, the railroad was altering the habitat of the buffalo, and beavers were getting more and more scarce because they were being over-trapped. Now, the buffalo was almost gone, and the dozens of tribes that depended on it were following it into oblivion.

If he looked hard enough, Chance told himself, there would be a reason, one he didn't see right off, which made sense, because he wasn't an Indian.

But it still didn't explain the whiskey. And that was what worried him. Whiskey was the white man's creation. White men made it and white men sold it. The Apache made *tizwin*, fermenting the mescal roots, and drinking themselves into three-day hangovers, but what he smelled had not been *tizwin*, it was bourbon. If the Apache he had just buried had gotten his hands on some whiskey, somewhere there was a white man involved, probably to make a dollar.

For Chance, though, that explanation was overridden by the single most important concern in his life: his family. Reasons were sometimes a luxury. And Dalton Chance could not afford luxury. He had all he could do to scratch a living from the hostile land he had chosen to live on. He wanted only to be left alone, to take care of his wife and boys. The Indian who lay under the neat array of stone had tried to damage that precarious balance, maybe for good reasons, but not for any reason Chance could accept. Jenny and the boys came first, and he would kill any man who tried to harm them.

The scary stories were everywhere, and at the bottom of each one was a simple fact. The Apaches were brutal. Whether they had a reason for it or not, the brutality itself could not be denied. And if something was happening at San Carlos, something that got out of control, they would all be in danger.

Knowing that did little to dispose him toward understanding. He was frightened, for himself and for his family, and fear makes men ugly. That was something else he had learned. He had learned it about himself in the most painful lesson, and he didn't like to think about it. There was brutality in him too, as much as he would like to pretend otherwise.

The first flush of terror behind him, he let the fear sink to the bottom of his consciousness like a rock in a murky pond. For the moment, he remembered it was there, but soon he would forget. And then it would begin to control him, to govern everything he did and everything he thought.

That scared him, too.

He tried to control the sense of impending upheaval. It was no big thing, he kept telling himself. One drunken warrior doesn't make a war. That's what he wanted to think. And that's what he would tell Jenny.

It was not what he knew to be true.

He didn't know anything. And the more he thought about it, the less certain he was. Pretending might be the best thing, and for a few minutes he had himself convinced he wouldn't tell Jenny anything at all. Not used to lying, the thought un-settled him. And he realized he would never be able to pull it off.

He would tell her the truth, and try to reassure her. She was a good woman, and she was strong. And probably had more courage than he had.

Probably so, he thought. Probably so.

3

AT SUNUP, Chance was already dressed. He had spent most of the night tossing and turning, smoking more than he was used to, and even poured himself two fingers of bourbon. The whiskey still sat on the table, untouched. Sitting there at the table, swirling the bourbon around in the glass, he realized the irony. Drinking whiskey as a reaction to being shot at by a man who had drunk too much made no sense.

He looked in on the kids every fifteen minutes, every time feeling that same chill down his spine. He kept hearing things, or imagining he did. Either way, it had the same effect. His Colt sat on the table, next to the glass of whiskey.

At five thirty, he picked up the Colt, tucked it in his belt, and stepped outside, just in time to watch the sun swell over the lip of the earth like a fat blood blister. Dark and ominous, it grew to huge proportions before climbing above the horizon and shrinking back to its normal size. It was going to be a scorcher.

Chance walked to the corral. The horses were nervous, too. All five of them pushed up against the rails as he approached, jockeying for position. He walked down the line swatting muzzle after muzzle, running his fingers through the stiff manes and talking to them in a soothing tone.

They settled down a little, but he wondered what had spooked them in the first place. Walking around the corral, he checked the ground for footprints, just in case. He didn't see anything out of the ordinary, certainly no moccasin prints. But he still wondered.

Chance walked to the barn. The door was open. He tried to remember whether he had closed it the night before, but drew a blank. Ordinarily, he never forgot to close it, but yesterday he might have. Yesterday had not been an ordinary day. Chance looked around the barn, his ears pricked for the least sound. He heard a mouse in the loft, maybe even a rat.

Or was it something a little larger?

Pulling the Colt from his belt, he walked to the ladder. "Anyone there?" he called.

There was no answer. But then, if someone were there, he could hardly expect an answer. "I'm coming up," he shouted. His hands were sweating and the Colt felt slippery. He changed hands, wiped his right palm on his shirt, then changed hands again.

When his head reached the level of the loft floor, he waited, listening. Whatever it was had stopped moving. He felt silly, but he had to check. He went up another rung, his eyes trying to pierce the gloom with indifferent success. He should have brought a lantern, he thought. Then shrugged. Up another rung, he was waist high in the loft now. Looking at every corner, he still saw nothing. And heard nothing.

He was about to climb all the way up, when he heard something below, outside. He dropped a rung and looked toward the door, then quickly went all the way down. He moved toward the door, cocking the hammer on the Colt and holding the gun so tightly his knuckles hurt.

At the doorway, he waited. Footsteps, ordinary footsteps, not those of someone trying to be quiet.

"Dalton?"

It was Jenny.

Chance sighed and stepped into the open. Jenny saw the pistol right away.

"What's wrong, hon?"

Chance sighed. He laughed unconvincingly. "A little skittish, that's all. Thought I heard something in the loft."

"What are you doing up so early?"

"Restless."

"You didn't sleep, did you?"

He didn't answer. But Jenny wasn't going to be put off.

"Dalton, I asked you a question."

"No, I didn't sleep."

"What are you going to do? You can't stay awake the rest of your life, you know?"

She wasn't being critical, but he was in no mood to be lectured on the obvious. "I know that, Jesus, Jenny. I'm just a little nervous, that's all."

"Maybe you should go see Sheriff Walker, tell him what happened. Maybe he knows something."

"I'm going to do just that, this afternoon."

"It can't have been anything serious," she said. "They would have sent a galloper to warn us. Probably just one of those things that happen. That's all it was."

"I want to believe that. But it wasn't just being shot at. It was *why* I was shot at. The Apache had been drinking. If he hadn't he probably would have killed me."

"If he hadn't been drinking, he probably wouldn't have shot at you in the first place."

"I guess. I'll go see Walker later. You need anything from town?"

"No, why?"

"I just thought you might. No reason. Thought you might want to come with me."

"And leave the children."

"Of course not. Bring them, too."

"We'll be alright, Dalton. Honestly, there's nothing to worry about."

"You don't know that."

"You don't know that we won't."

Jenny shook her head. "We have lives to lead, Dalton. Normal lives. If this is where we're going to live, then we better learn to adjust. We've been here three years, already, and this is the first time anything like this has happened."

"Suppose it's not the last?"

"Then we'll deal with it. Right now, I'd just as soon go on as we have been."

Chance walked away a few steps. He looked up at the sun, already changing color, the orangey light beginning to brighten to yellow. In a couple of hours, it would be white. He turned back to his wife.

"You're right, I guess, Jenny. I just worry, that's all. I mean, if anything ever happened to you or the kids . . ."

"Nothing will happen. You just go talk to Sheriff Walker this morning. I'm sure he'll handle it."

Chance shook his head. "Yeah, I guess so."

"Why don't you go in and lie down for awhile. I'll make breakfast later. The boys can handle the chores this morning. They're getting old enough now, they probably ought to be doing it anyway."

"They're too young yet. They'll have to work the rest of their lives. Why not let them enjoy the little time they have?"

"We'll talk about it later. Just this once won't hurt them any."

Jenny grabbed him by the arm, linked hers around his, and started to pull him toward the house. He resisted at first, but he was exhausted. And deep down, he knew Jenny was probably right. A little sleep would help calm his nerves, let him see things more clearly.

He didn't want to charge into Walker's office like some hysteric. Not that folks around here tended to be calm about Apaches. The very mention of the name provoked everything from a nervous tic to language unsuitable for mixed company. It bothered him to see people that close to panic. The last thing he wanted was to become just like them. But, God knew, he had more reason than most, after the events of the previous day.

He stayed on the porch for a minute after Jenny went in. Looking around at his small holdings, he was struck by just how precarious their existence was.

The land itself was forbidding and hostile. It was beautiful, but the beauty was remote, and had little to do with the presence of man. Water was scarce throughout the territory, except for the valleys of the few rivers, and an occasional spring.

The sun was brutal for more than half the year, and could kill a man in hours in the dead of summer.

And hovering over all of it was the threat of the Apaches. The Indians weren't that numerous, maybe twenty thousand if all the groups were counted, and some, like the Warm Springs and the White Mountain Apaches, were less hostile than others. But the Chiricahua and Bedonkohe seemed to take their temper from the land itself. They were fierce and fiercely independent, more brutal than the sun, deadlier than anything that crept or crawled over the deserts or haunted the barren mountains.

And they were more cruel than any other tribe, even the Sioux and the Comanche. He'd seen his share of brutality, but there was nothing in his experience to compare with the stories the old timers here liked to tell. And he didn't doubt a single one of them.

But it was home, and he'd be damned if anybody was going to take it away from him. He wasn't that young anymore. He didn't have that many good years left, too damned few to pull up stakes and start all over again someplace else. This was his home, and he planned to die here, be buried under the little stand of cottonwoods down by the south fork of Bitter Creek.

Not too soon, he hoped, but someday. When the

boys were grown, able to fend for themselves, he wouldn't mind lying down one night and not getting up in the morning. That was the way to go, peacefully, in his own bed, surrounded by the family he loved. But not yet, not for a while yet, he whispered.

He turned and went inside, letting the door hit him in the back as he entered. Jenny wasn't in the kitchen. He knew where she would be, and he tiptoed to the back of the cabin. And he was right. She stood at the foot of the bed, her hands locked together, fingers intertwined, almost as if she had been praying but was too self-conscious to fold her hands outright.

He stepped to her side and wrapped an arm around her waist. They stood for a long moment, looking down at the two boys, Dalton Junior and Curt, named for her grandfather.

Jenny laid her hand on his shoulder. "They're so beautiful," she whispered. "And so young."

Chance tugged her away gently. She resisted for a moment, then followed him. He led her to the other bedroom, where they could talk without waking the boys. A coal oil lamp, its wick turned most of the way down, glowed dimly on the small table next to the bed.

For the first time, he noticed the dampness around her eyes, the little golden trails down her cheeks, where the tears picked up the lamplight, and reflected it back. He reached out with a thumb and wiped the two streams away.

"I get so scared," she said, sucking in her breath, and letting it out in a single, trembling stream. "I feel so helpless, sometimes."

"We don't have to stay here," he said.

"Yes, we do."

"No, we don't. Jenny, if you're not happy here, we can find someplace else. It would be hard, but . . ."

"Too hard, Dalton. We just can't pick up and go."

"Is that what you want, though?"

"I don't know. Maybe. I just . . ." She let her words trail off until there was nothing but silence in the room with them. He could hear her breathing, and his own. He wanted to say something to reassure her, but he didn't know what to say.

Jenny pushed him gently toward the bed. "Lie down," she said.

He did as he was told. She bent to pull his boots off, but he shook his head. "Leave them," he said.

Jenny took a blanket and draped it over him, tucking it around his shoulders. "I'll wake you in a couple of hours."

Chance nodded. The last thing he saw was Jenny backing toward the door, the little shining smears on her cheeks almost gone now. He closed his eyes, sighed once, and was asleep.

4

COTTON SPRINGS WASN'T much to look at. Half the buildings in the town had never seen a paint brush, and the other half didn't need it. They were made of adobe and logs. You used what came to hand to build anything out here. Chance pulled up on the hilltop overlooking the town. In the back of his mind was the idea that it could become something, a place they could all be proud of, a place to raise families. They could build a school, maybe a church or two.

But right now, the truth was he didn't much care for what he saw. The arid climate was a kind of blessing here. The towns in Kansas and Wyoming he'd seen, the Nebraska cow towns and the mining towns in Colorado all suffered from an excess of mud. Paving was for eastern city sissies. But a heavy rain and two hundred horses can fill a town with muck in nothing flat, half mud and half horse-shit, you could probably cut and dry blocks out of the filthy mess and build something down here.

But Cotton Springs was what it was. And right now, it was his home. He kicked the pony once, too easily, then again, this time making sure the horse understood. Moving downhill, he stared across the roofs at the red rock beyond it and, beyond that, the long horizontal smear of purple that marked the mountains to the south.

Little puffs of dust, kicked up by the pony's hooves, swirled on the hot wind, the fine particles of sand hissing as they scoured the rocks and sifted through the chollo and saguaro. It sounded dry, it looked dry, and he was so damn thirsty, he was dry, too. The sun was almost blinding. Nearly straight overhead, it turned everything a bone white shade or, like the cactus, a gray green, as if it were bleaching everything even as he looked at it.

He was soaked through with sweat, and his hands hurt. Tanned to bronze even though they were, they felt the sting of heat. It had to be a hundred and ten, maybe a little more. He could check at the General Store, if Mosely's new thermometer was in. The last one had been broken by a drunken cowboy, who ripped the fragile glass off the wooden mount and stuck it in his mouth. But he bit down too hard and swallowed enough mercury to kill half a dozen men.

Or so the story went. Whatever the truth, Mosely had the only thermometer in town, and when it got broken, people spent more than the usual amount of time talking about the heat, mostly because nobody knew anything for sure.

Chance tilted his hat down even further over his eyes, and eased the pony into a walk as he neared the edge of town. The handlettered sign, its paint almost flaked off by the intense heat over the past eight years, gave the population as two hundred and eleven. But that was stretching it, Chance thought. Maybe on a Friday or Saturday night. And maybe not even then.

The streets, both of them, were deserted. Horses, the heat too much for them even to switch their tails, sat docilely at a half-dozen hitching posts scattered down the main street. And they were the only sign of life.

As he got closer, Chance heard a piano tinkling somewhere, probably at Red Malone's saloon. The piano was badly out of tune, but the kind of clients who frequented Malone's place were unlikely to notice. Music was just about the last thing on their minds. But it bothered him to hear the sour notes. Jenny played so prettily, and their own piano, hauled all the way from Independence, sounded a hell of a lot better, even though it hadn't been tuned in nearly two years. The last time the tuner passed through, Chance hadn't had the money.

Next time, he would. He'd been squirreling it away in a tobacco tin in the barn. It might be six months or a year before the tuner came back, but Chance would be ready.

Reining in in front of the Sheriff's office, Chance sat his horse for a long moment, giving the piano one last chance. The piano player, probably Curly Sloan, was doing his best to work his way through a Stephen Foster thing, but Chance wasn't sure of the name of it. Hell, he thought, with that cater-wauling, it's hard enough to recognize whether it's Foster at all.

He slipped from the saddle, trying to tune out the jangling of the instrument, and looped his reins around the post. The front door was closed, but that was just to keep the worst of the hot wind out. Walker should be there. It was nearly one o'clock.

He tried the knob, it turned, and he pushed the door open. Jim Slattery, the deputy, was asleep be-hind the desk. Chance knocked, but Slattery just snored a little louder. Chance rapped again, this time using his knuckles on the gold leaf lettering on the glass.

This time, Slattery snorted and jerked his head up. "The hell is goin' on?"

He looked at Chance, blinked his eyes, then rubbed them with his knuckles. Looking again, this time he recognized the visitor.

"Oh, it's you, Chance. How you doin'?"

"Not bad, Jim. The Sheriff around?"

"Problem?"

"I don't know. I guess I want to ask the Sheriff that very question."

"He's over to Malone's, I think. There was some trouble there, and he had to break up a fight."

"This early?"

"You know how it is. Red don't water his whiskey. Some folks ain't used to that. Sheriff probably hung around awhile to make sure things don't get goin' again too soon."

"Guess I'll take a walk over. Could use a drink myself."

"Me too, but I can't drink on duty. Unfortunate, ain't it?"

Chance laughed. "For who?"

"Hell, for me, who else?"

"Thought maybe you worked better with a wet whistle."

"No sir, not me. But used to be a deputy hereabouts, around five six years ago, back before you came. Used to break open a bottle at daybreak. Did good work, though. Never seemed to bother him none."

"What happened to him?"

"Apaches got him. He was lucky, though. They just shot him. They like to half skinned the fella was with him. The army didn't come along, they mighta done that to Bob, too. That was his name, Bob Randall. Nice fella, he was."

"You take it easy, Slats. I don't find the Sheriff, you tell him I'll be by later, alright?"

"Sure thing, Dalton. But you'll find him right enough. Probably asleep in Malone's back room. Say hello to Jenny and them boys of yours. She alright?"

"Sure, why?"

Chance tensed up as he turned back to Slattery.

"No reason. Ain't seen her in awhile, is all. She sure is a pretty thing, that Jenny. You're a lucky man, Dalton."

He relaxed at that. "I know it. See you later."

Chance pushed back into the hot street, reluctantly. He stood on the wooden walk a minute then, not knowing what else to do, started to Red Malone's saloon.

The damned piano was jangling worse than ever, but it was the only sound. Whatever had required the presence of Tommy Walker seemed to have died down and stayed dead. Chance pushed the doors of the saloon aside, spreading his arms to keep them from springing back and hitting him before he got through.

A half dozen men sat at the bar, three or four more at one of the round tables scattered around the floor. At the piano in the corner, a man he'd never seen, wearing a straw hat and a red and white striped shirt, with fancy sleeve garters, was banging away at the keys. He wondered what happened to Curly Sloan.

Malone waved. "Howdy, Dalton. What're you drinkin'?"

"Nothing, Red, thanks. Just looking for Tom Walker. He around?"

"Was in earlier. Had to ride out to Jasper Green's place, though. Trouble?"

"Not really. Not now, anyhow."

"Old Jasper come rippin' in here like the devil was in his pocket. Should have seen him. Claimed an Apache was sneakin' around his spread yesterday."

"What'd the Sheriff say?"

"Said Jasper was crazy, what do you think he said?"

"I'm not so sure of that, Red."

"Oh come on, Dalton. Not you, too. Must be something in the water. Maybe you should have a beer, wash it out of your system."

"Too late for that, Red."

"What happened?"

"Nothing much. No need to go into it."

"Tom left about twenty minutes ago. You can probably still catch him, you feel the need. You know where Green's place is?"

Chance nodded. "Thanks, Red. Think I might do that."

He nodded to a couple of farmers he knew and walked back into the street. He debated whether or not to go after Walker, then decided that if Jasper Green saw something, it might be important for Tom to know what happened yesterday. He broke into a half trot, mounted up in a hurry and pushed his horse on through town. Green lived down south of Cotton Springs, in the other direction from his own place. The sooner he caught up with Walker, the shorter his ride home would be.

Almost by instinct, he reached for the Colt on his hip, just to make sure it was still there. It was.

But he didn't feel any better knowing it.

Walker wouldn't be pushing his horse very hard in this heat, so he had a decent chance to catch him before he'd gone more than two or three miles. That is, unless Jasper was pushing things. That would be just like him, too, Chance thought.

Green had a reputation as something of an alarmist. He never saw an Indian that wasn't an Apache, and never saw an Apache under seven feet tall. To hear Green describe one of his sightings, you'd think all Indians were super-human sized with blood dripping from their mouths and a half dozen scalps in each hand, even though scalping wasn't generally practiced by the Apaches. The last thing Chance wanted was to get lumped in with a fanatic like Jasper Green.

But what happened to him the day before had

been the real thing. It was a real Apache, and he was really dead. And that was a fact.

The road to Jasper Green's place wound through some pretty country, but Chance wasn't interested in sightseeing. He wanted just one thing—to find Tom Walker and tell him what happened. After that, it would be up to the Sheriff.

Fifteen minutes of hard riding brought him to the south of Deerleg Canyon. Walker was still nowhere in sight. Chance wondered whether it was worth the trouble. But he knew it was. He sighed and kicked the horse a little harder, heading into the canyon at a fast trot. Halfway through, he saw two riders, Green and the Sheriff, probably. The canyon bent to the left two thirds of the way through, giving it its name. In a couple of hundred yards, the two men would make the turn and they'd be out of sight again. They were too far to hear him clearly if he shouted. The best thing to do would be get their attention, make them wait until he caught up.

Chance pulled his Colt and fired it into the air. Standing in the stirrups, he waved his hat over his head. Somebody, probably Walker, waved back, and he saw the two riders turn their mounts before he dropped back to the saddle and urged his own horse on. A flash of light caught his attention high on the rimrock. It puzzled him for a moment.

He watched for it to be repeated, but nothing

happened. A moment later, a gunshot cracked from almost the same spot. Chance hauled his Winchester from its boot and reined in. He could see the Sheriff looking back over his shoulder, and Green beating it toward him at a full gallop.

A second shot echoed off the canyon walls, and he saw a spout of sand kick up a few yards ahead of Green. Then it got quiet.

Chance dismounted and took cover behind a slab of red rock. The two riders came on, charging hard. He saw another flash, this time well down the face of the canyon wall. He steeled himself for another rifle shot, but it never came. The range was too long. Walker waved his hat again, closed fast and skidded to a halt right behind Jasper.

"Dalton, what the hell is going on?"

"That's what I want to talk to you about, Sheriff."

"Good thing you did. You just might have saved our asses. That bushwhacker would have had us dead to rights."

"That weren't no bushwhacker, Sheriff," Green said. " I told you. Apaches. You see if I ain't right."

"Come on, Jasper. You been worrying too much again."

"No sir. I know what I know."

Walker looked at Chance. "Old Jasper's been seeing Apaches, he says. Says they was around his spread last night. I told him he's crazy, but he says I got to come see. But you know what I reckon? I

reckon old Jasper's done found hisself a pair of
Apache moccasins. Probably had a few drinks, run
around the corral in 'em, then kept on goin'
around and around. Every time around, he found
a few more tracks. Two thousand Indians out there
now."

Walker laughed.

Chance just looked at him. "Jasper just might be
right, Sheriff."

"Oh, come on, Dalton. Not you, too?"

"Yup."

5

JASPER GREEN'S PLACE was tucked in against the base of a wall of red stone. Not too close, to be safe from the great flakes of rock that broke off without warning. A sharp crack like small thunder in the middle of the night often signalled that another slab was coming down, then the big thunder of the fall itself. But it was close enough to get some shade from the worst of the afternoon sun. A stand of cottonwoods fanned out behind the house, offering a little more shade.

The corral was a typical affair, hand-split logs, rough hewn and carefully shaped on the ends to fit into the slots cut through the posts. It seemed an appendage of the ramshackle barn. Jasper Green was never a calm man, but now he seemed on the edge of frenzy, as he urged Chance and the Sheriff to dismount. "Check over there, around the back end," he said for the fourth time since they reached the corral. "I'm telling you, them's Apaches moccasin prints. Look at the damn toe. That's all you need to see."

Walker looked at Chance, shrugged and dismounted. Chance slipped from his own saddle and followed the Sheriff around the corner of the fence.

"Don't be steppin' on 'em," Green shouted. He had stayed on his horse, his carbine braced across the saddle horn, as if the very prints, if they were Apache, would be lethal to the unwary. Walker shook his head, a man humoring a frantic child, but he moved away from the fence a little, and slowed his pace.

At the next corner, he stopped. Green shouted for him to move down along the fence a few yards, but Walker waved a hand. "Just a damn minute, Jasper. I can't think straight with all your jabbering. Hold your water."

He looked at Chance. "Dalton," he said, "before I go looking for something that probably ain't there, you mind telling me what you meant back there at Deerleg?"

"Like I said, Tom, somebody took a couple shots at me, over by Bald Mesa. Yesterday afternoon."

"And you think it was an Apache?"

"I know it was, Tom."

"Why you so sure?"

"Because I buried him, Sheriff. With my own hands." Chance looked at his upturned palms as if expecting there to be some visible proof graven into the skin.

"You what? You killed him?"

"No. Oh I would've, sure enough, if I had to, but he did himself in, before it came to that. Fell off the damn mesa and damn near split himself open like a goddamn cantaloupe."

"And he was Apache. You're sure of that?"

"No question. Thing is, Tom, he was drinking. And I know the reservation is off limits for whiskey. But he was drunk as a skunk. Lost his balance when he come after me. I was halfway up and he came on over the top and down. Fell like a rotten apple. Lost his balance, that's why I think he was drunk. From what I hear, an Apache can walk on a thread between two hills."

"Unless he's liquored up, you mean . . . *Tizwin*, maybe?"

"Whiskey, Tom. No doubt about it. Bourbon, I think."

"You think he was drunk on white man's liquor?"

"I do. And he was. What I wanted to know, you hear anything about any bucks leaving San Carlos?"

"Nope, I ain't Dalton. Not a word. Course, I tried to telegraph this morning, but the line's down."

"Or cut . . ."

"Hurry up, Sheriff, before the damn wind blows them prints away," Green shouted.

"Hush the hell up, Jasper, would you?" Walker scowled at the rancher for a second before turning back to Chance. "Maybe I ought to go on over and talk to Crook's people, see can they tell me anything. Let me take a look at these phantom footprints, and we'll talk about it."

Walker took a few steps, bent over at the waist, and studied the ground. "Wish to hell there'd been some rain," he said. "I ain't much of a tracker. And if a redskin don't want you to know he's been around, it takes a hell of a lot better eye than mine to see any sign."

Chance joined him, then dropped to one knee. He, too, leaned forward, bringing his cheek almost to the ground level. "I can see something," he said. "Footprint, too, for sure."

"Hell, Dalton, you got to be half Indian your own self you can see something on this ground."

"It's there, alright."

"You and Jasper been pullin' on the same jug, ain't you?" Walker laughed. Chance didn't join him.

"You wouldn't be laughin' so hard, Tom, it was you that got shot at yesterday."

"Hell, Dalton, I got shot at this morning, remember?"

Chance nodded. "Who did the shooting, you think about that?"

"No Apache, that's for sure."

"I'm not sure of that, Tom. Not sure at all." Chance moved a couple of feet along the fence. "Here, look at this," he said, pointing at another depression in the dry soil, this one much more clearly defined.

Walker crept up alongside and leaned close to the ground. "I see that one, alright. Maybe you and Jasper are right," Walker said. He stroked his chin thoughtfully. "You up for a long ride?"

"I got to tell Jenny, first."

"I'll send Slats out to your place, he can tell her. We should be back by sundown. We got to pass through town anyhow. It'll save time."

"Alright. I guess it might not be a bad idea."

"I still think we're worrying about nothing, mind you, but all the same . . ." He let the thought trail off, and Chance didn't need anyone to finish it. Walker was alluding to the horror they might all face if there was anything to the suspicion that some of the Apaches had, indeed, broken out of the reservation. They had done it before, and the results had been bloody, to say the least. Walker wasn't pleased at the prospect that it might happen again, that much was clear.

The Sheriff stood up. "Jasper, come on over here." He walked to the end of the fence and waited for Green to meet him. "You lose anything last night?"

"I already told you, six horses."

"Anything else?"

Green shook his head. "No guns, nothing like that. Just the ponies. But they were good horses."

"I'm not talking about value, Jasper, I'm talking about use to an Apache."

"Nope, nothing else." Green looked pleased. "You believe me now, don't you Sheriff? Thought I was imagining things, I know that. But I wasn't."

"I wish to hell you were, Jasper. I can tell you that much. Listen, you keep an eye peeled. Me and Dalton are gonna go have a talk with General Crook, see if he can tell us anything."

"Crook's a damn Indian lover, Tom, you know that. Hell, he uses more Apaches than he does white men."

"He gets results, though, doesn't he, Jasper?" Chance had an edge to his voice, and Green noticed. "Christ almighty. I forgot. Dalton, you know I didn't mean nothing, it's just that . . ."

"I know what you meant, Jasper. I heard it often enough up in Wyoming."

"Nobody said nothing about you personally, Dalton," Green said. "Didn't mean nothing, either."

Chance shook his head. "General Crook knows what he's doing. The fact is, the Army doesn't always get told. Sometimes there's trouble on a reservation, and the Agent tries to patch things up himself. Most times it works. Sometimes it doesn't. It's the sometimes we got to worry about. If some of the Apaches have jumped, Crook ought to know. If he doesn't, he'll sure as hell find out, you can bet on that."

"I'm more worried about the whiskey angle," Walker said.

"What whiskey angle?" Green said.

"Dalton here was near killed by a drunk Apache yesterday."

"That's that damn Wiley," Green said. "I already told you about that two or three times, Tom. Ain't you done nothing about it yet?"

"Can't do anything without proof, Jasper, you know that."

"Hell, Tom, you're the Sheriff. Gettin' proof is part of your damned job, ain't it?"

"What do you want me to do?" Walker snapped. "Make it myself. I already told you, I can't find anything."

"Then look again, goddamn it. We got families here."

"Who's Wiley?" Chance asked. "What's this all about?"

"Tucker Wiley, runs a general supply outfit over to Dry Gap. Big time operation."

"He's a damn leech, that's what he is," Green

snarled. "Sells stuff on the reservation, and gets fat on army supply contracts at the same time. That's how he gets the damn whiskey to the Indians. Then, when they go hog wild, the army gets called in to fix it, and he makes more money yet. Blood-sucking bastard. Gonna get more white folks killed, and he don't give a damn."

"You know he's selling whiskey at San Carlos?" Chance asked.

"Hell, yes, I know it. So does any one-eyed man in Arizona's got half a brain in his head."

"What's that make me, Jasper?" Walker asked quietly.

"Sheriff, I guess," Green said. He didn't mean it as a joke. And Tom Walker didn't take it as one.

6

FORT APACHE SPRAWLED across several acres of flat, dry as dust land within sight of the blue-black and red walls of the Gila Mountains to the south. Cookie cutter wooden barracks, more than a dozen of them, formed a large square. One side of the square looked more substantial than the other three, because it included the administrative buildings for the fort, as well as supply and magazine storage.

When they rode in, nobody paid any attention to Chance and Walker. A handful of enlisted men lounged at one corner of the porch running the length of the headquarters, others tended to a variety of business from unloading supplies to picket duty on the perimeter. It looked more peaceful than Chance expected. If anything had happened at San Carlos, there was no sign of it here.

They tied up at the hitching post in front of the main building, and Chance climbed the two steps to the porch, then waited for the Sheriff. Walker stood with his hands on his hips, surveying the broad, open court. He watched a detail busily reassembling a small howitzer. The men were laughing and joking while they worked, snapping oily rags at one another and acting for all the world like schoolboys, not soldiers.

Walker climbed onto the porch with a grunt. "Getting old, Dalton," he said. "This country takes a lot out of a man my age."

Chance laughed. "Makes a man my age feel like a man your age, Sheriff," he said.

"You ready to beard the lion in his den?"

"Why not?"

A corporal, his wide stripes newly sewn on a uniform that had seen better days but still looked spic and span, watched them with tilted head. "Can I help you gentlemen?" he asked.

"Like to see General Crook, if he's around."

"Yes sir. He's in his office. This way, please." The corporal led them through the door. Inside, three noncoms shuffled papers at a long table, another sat behind a battle-scarred wooden desk. None of them looked up. Crook was famous for his insistence on orderliness and they were too close to the General's office to run the risk of being anything but efficient.

The corporal headed for an open door at the back side of the large room. He waved for them to follow, then stopped about fifteen feet from the doorway. "May I ask your names and your business?"

Walker said, "I'm Tom Walker, Sheriff of Cotton Springs, over in Flores County, and this is Dalton Chance. But I'd rather tell the general himself why we're here, if you don't mind, Corporal."

The corporal nodded. "Yes sir. Wait here a moment, please, I'll see if the General is free."

When he disappeared through the open door, it closed behind him. "Never yet seen a brass hat was free, Dalton," Walker whispered. "You?"

"Crook's different."

"I know that. Some say he's crazy, too. That don't mean he's free."

Chance smiled distantly. His mind was back at Cotton Springs. He wondered how Jenny and the boys were holding up. They had to be worried; he just hoped they weren't too upset.

The Corporal reopened the door and summoned them with a wave. He announced them, and stepped aside for the visitors to enter, then pulled the door closed behind him as he returned to his post.

The General was busy scrawling his signature on a stack of papers, and didn't bother to look up until he was finished. He stuck the pen back in the ink pot, sat back in his chair and smiled. "I didn't expect I'd ever see you again, Sergeant," he said.

Walker cleared his throat. "That's Sheriff, General, I'm Sheriff over in . . ."

"I know that. I was talking to Mr. Chance."

Chance shook his head. "I didn't think you'd remember me, General." He moved closer to shake hands.

"I remember every man who ever served with me." Chance noted the preposition, thinking it was as apt a capsule of the man as any. Most would have said "under." Crook smiled again. "Still got that grip, eh?" He turned to Walker. "Sorry, Sheriff, but old times are precious to a man my age."

Walker shook hands. "I didn't realize you two were acquainted," he said. "Pleased to meet you."

"Now, what can I do for you?"

Walker looked at Chance, debating which of them should speak first. Chance nodded back. Walker cleared his throat again. "Well, we don't want to sound like we're raising a fuss about nothing, General, but we were wondering if anything's going on over to San Carlos, the reservation."

Crook sucked his cheeks in and stroked his beard. For a moment, the only sound was the squeak of his chair. "Such as?"

"Well, whether maybe some of them bucks has left the reservation."

Crook looked thoughtful. "Why do you ask?"
he said.

"Somebody, an Apache actually, tried to kill
Chance yesterday. Then a local rancher, fella
named Green, found footprints, moccasin prints,
around his corral. Claims it was an Apache, at
least one, maybe more. Jasper's a bit excitable,
see."

Crook looked at Chance. "Sergeant, why don't
you tell me exactly what happened?"

Chance did. Crook didn't like what he heard.
He didn't say anything for a long time. When he
did speak, he glanced at the closed door. His voice
was low. "You say the Apache is dead, Chance?"

"Yes, sir. I didn't kill him, though. He just lost
his footing. I guess I would have, though, if it came
to that."

"How he died won't make much difference.
That he's dead will make all the difference in the
world."

"What do you mean, General?" Walker asked.

"The Apache are funny about this sort of thing.
They take warfare seriously, more than any other
Indians I know. Somebody will be using this as an
excuse, maybe already has."

"So you do know something." The way Chance
put it, it clearly was a conclusion, not a question.

"Not for certain," Crook said. "But there have
been rumors the last couple, three days. I sent a de-

tachment over to San Carlos to talk to Mitchell, but I haven't heard anything yet."

"Mitchell the agent?"

Crook nodded. "A good man, but he bends over backwards for the Apache. Too far, and too damn often."

"So you think there's going to be trouble?"

"There's already trouble, Chance. A man's dead. Doesn't matter how or why. We can't change it. If this isn't nipped, and soon, we could have a full-fledged rebellion on our hands. Some of the chiefs are none too happy with things, and it won't take much to push them over the edge. If that happens, they'll take off for Mexico, and I don't want to think about what might happen between here and there. And neither do you."

"Can't their grievances be addressed?" Chance asked.

"They're Indians," Walker reminded him, "they don't have a right to any grievances."

Crook frowned without speaking. He tilted his head to one side and made a tent of his fingers. Peering through them, he appeared to be measuring Walker for some indefinable quality. He obviously didn't like what he saw.

"That's exactly the problem, Sheriff," he said. He lowered his hands and looked Walker square in the eye. "They *do* have a right, only nobody seems to give a good God damn."

"You're new here, General," Walker said. "I been here for a dozen years, a little longer. I know what it was like back in the early seventies. I seen women raped to death, children with their throats cut. Found a man one time, his damn heart cut out. We found the heart, too, lyin' in the sand. Looked like somebody took a damn bite out of it."

"You say you've been here twelve years . . ."

"Give or take, yes."

"Tell me, Sheriff Walker, was there anyone here when you arrived?"

"A few folks, yeah. Hell, I ain't no hermit. Wouldn't have stopped unless there was someplace *to* stop."

"Where were the Apaches, then?"

Walker realized what Crook was getting at, but he waved a hand as if to push the question aside. "That don't count, General. I'm talking about white men."

"I'm talking about the land, Sheriff, the land itself, with all of its beauty and all of its ugliness. I'm talking about the people who lived here before you, hell, before you were even born. Before even the Spanish had come."

"Times change, General. It's a new day. There's lots of folks back east pushing on us. We need room."

"What about the Apaches? Don't they need room?"

"I reckon so."

"Then why is it so hard to understand the problem? How would you feel if strange men by the thousands showed up in your backyard one morning, and told you you had to move on, that they needed, or at least wanted, your land, and that they would find someplace else for you to live?"

"You sound more like a preacher than a soldier."

"No. I *am* a soldier. And I have a job to do. But you have to know your enemy if you expect to succeed, and a good soldier knows that fighting should be the last resort. When all else fails, that's when you turn to the sword, Sheriff. Not before."

"Seems like to me, General, that all else has already failed. One of them Apaches tried to kill Chance, here. A couple more took a shot at me and Jasper Green this morning."

"You saw them?"

"Well, hell, yeah, I guess so. We . . ."

"Did you actually see who shot at you, Sheriff?"

Walker sighed. "Not exactly, no."

"Then how do you know it was an Apache? Might it have been a Navajo? A Hopi? Maybe it was a Kiowa? Maybe a Comanche? Why, for all you know, Sheriff, it might even have been a white man . . ." Crook leaned forward in his chair. Its squeak was the only sound in the room.

Walker looked at Chance, who shrugged.

"Isn't that so, Sheriff?" Crook persisted.

"It was an Apache tried to kill Chance. He's got the body to prove it. Leastways he did have. Maybe it's not there, now."

"Whether it is or not, does it prove an Apache shot at you this morning?"

"No, it doesn't prove an Apache shot at me this morning. But it stands to reason, General."

"No it doesn't, Sheriff. It's just supposition. However logical it might be, it's no more than supposition. I can't afford to act on supposition."

"So I suppose you won't do nothing about it. Is that what you're trying to say?"

"No, not exactly. What I'm trying to say is I need more information, I need facts, not guesses. I'm trying to gather that information, but it takes time."

"Time is something we ain't got much of, General. The way I look at it. We're pretty near out of time."

"Don't do anything rash, Sheriff. I understand your anxiety, but you could make the situation a lot worse by doing something provocative."

"What about the whiskey, General?" Chance asked.

"We've heard the rumors. We're trying to pin them down, but it takes time."

"Tucker Wiley's the name I heard. You look at him close?"

" I know Mr. Wiley. He is a very ambitious man, Sergeant, but I don't think he's a fool."

"That makes him even more dangerous, then, doesn't it?"

"Possibly. But I don't know anything that would lead me to believe he is in any way involved in this."

"Have you asked him?"

Crook nodded.

"And what does he say?"

"He denies it."

"And you accept that?" Walker snorted. "Hell, I never arrested a guilty man yet, General. You don't believe me, just ask them. They're all innocent."

"I don't take this lightly, Sheriff. I can assure you of that. If Tucker Wiley is doing anything he's not supposed to, I'll find out about it. And he'll be dealt with. I'll let you know what I find out. About the whiskey, and about the renegades. If there are any."

"There are, alright, General," Walker said. "And when you count 'em up, minus one. Dalton here," he jerked a thumb at Chance, "did the subtractin'."

7

WHEN CHANCE LEFT the General's office, he noticed an Apache sitting by the door. The man wore a Cavalry tunic, but otherwise was indistinguishable from any other Apache. Chance glanced at him and the man stared back with impassive features. Black eyes, like two pieces of obsidian, glittered under the red sweatband. He sat quietly, with his hands folded in his lap, but he was conscious of everything going on around him.

Chance started to say something, then stopped. Walker noticed the Apache and pulled Chance by the arm. "Come on," Dalton," he said. "Let's go over to the trading post. Martha wants me to pick up some kind of cloth. I was supposed to bring it home tonight, but Wilson'll be closed up tight by the time we get back to Cotton Springs. I got a sample in my pocket, so I guess I'll see can I get it here."

Chance followed the Sheriff, but kept glancing back at the Indian, who followed him with his eyes. Chance had the impression that the man wanted to say something to him, but Walker was impatient, and Chance didn't want to make a fool of himself.

Outside, it was still hot. Little swirls of dust curled across the parade ground. The artillery crew had finished with its work, and the field pieces glittered in the sun. As they walked down the wooden walk, shielded from the sun by the split shake ramada overhead, Chance listened to the sound of his boots on the rough boards. Crook was right. He knew that, but it didn't make it any easier to swallow.

He could feel the tension inside him, squirming like a live thing. He wanted to do something with his hands, or run, anything to drain off some of the nervousness. When they got to the trading post, Walker reached into his pocket and pulled out a tattered scrap of red and white cloth. He waved it under Chance's nose. "See this, Dalton, this is what a woman can do to you. Here I am, traipsing halfway across hell to buy a bolt of calico. What in hell's wrong with me?"

"You're a husband, Tom." Chance laughed. "That's what husbands do."

"It's a damn shame, that's what it is. Errand boy for the missus, like I worked in a damn tailor shop."

Walker shook his head, then pushed on inside. Chance followed him toward the door, lagging behind a few feet. He looked down the walk, and saw the Apache standing in front of General Crook's headquarters, watching him.

Chance walked back to the edge of the walkway, dropped the two feet to the ground, then sat on the boards. He pulled a tobacco pouch from his shirt pocket and opened it casually. Unfolding a rolling paper, he poured a little too much tobacco onto it, tilted a little back and leveled it off. Rolling a little too quickly, he licked the edge and stuck the rudely finished cigarette in his mouth.

He lit it with a wooden match, snapped the match, an old army habit, and flicked the two pieces onto the dusty ground. Only when he had taken the first drag did he look toward the Apache. The scout was now standing beside him, and Chance hadn't even realized it.

He looked up and the Indian nodded. Stepping gracefully to the ground he sat squatted on his haunches and looked up at Chance.

"Gerardo," he said.

"What?" Chance was confused.

"Gerardo. That is the name of the man you buried."

"You were listening," Chance said.

The Apache nodded. "But I already knew. I saw you bury him."

"You were with him?"

The Indian shook his head. "I was looking for him."

"Why did he do it?"

The Indian mimed drinking from a bottle. "He was always a bad one. When he drank, he was worse. Many are like that. And many are looking for a reason to do what they already want to do."

"You're saying the whiskey was an excuse? Is that what you mean?"

"No. Not an excuse. I don't know the word, but I know what I mean."

"Why were you looking for him?"

"Because I knew he had the whiskey. I wanted to take it away from him before . . ."

"Before he did something stupid." Chance finished.

"Stupid is okay. Dangerous is not. Gerardo, and a lot of the others, don't understand."

"Understand what?"

"The old ways are dead. Long time now, we Apache have been calling ourselves *Indeh*. He knows this."

"*Indeh*?"

The Indian nodded. "*Indeh*. 'The Dead Ones.' Gerardo knows this, but he doesn't understand why. Not truly."

"Why are you telling me all this?"

The Indian didn't answer right away. He looked off at the sun. Chance noticed a single stalk of straw in the Apache's hand, its furred end trailing in the dust. The Apache tapped his knee with the stalk a couple of times. Then he looked at Chance. "I don't know," he said.

"Do you know where Gerardo got the whiskey?"

The Indian nodded.

"Will you tell me?"

"Not now."

"Why?"

No answer. Instead, he straightened up and stood looking down at Chance for a long moment. His broad features were as impressive as ever. The long, straight black hair picked up the sunlight and shimmered a little in the hot breeze. He was larger than Chance had thought, nearly six feet tall. His heavy legs and thick arms gave the impression of power rather than speed.

"What's your name?" Chance asked. "Will you tell me that, at least?"

"Ki-Lo-Tah. But the soldiers call me Lone Wolf. Because the Apaches call all Army scouts wolves."

"Have some of the bucks left the reservation?"

Lone Wolf looked at Chance for a long time. It seemed to Chance that he might not have heard the question and then, perhaps, that he had forgotten it. But he heard, and he didn't forget. He nodded. "Many."

"And General Crook doesn't know?"

"No."

"Are you going to tell him?"

Again, Lone Wolf waited a long time before answering. Chance wondered whether he was translating the question into his own language, framing an answer and then translating the answer into English. It seemed roundabout, but maybe it was the best way to avoid misunderstanding.

Lone Wolf sighed. "I am Apache," he said. "I sign papers that say I am in the army. So I am both an Apache and a soldier."

"It's difficult for you, hard, I know, but . . ."

"You don't know. I eat army food. But those on the reservation, they don't eat well. The meat is bad, and there is not as much as there is supposed to be. The white man wants the Apache to be a farmer, but there is no good land on the reservation. Woods and mountains, yes, but not good farmland. And they keep changing things. The grain is bad, the flour is full of insects. Not good. Not a good life to have for an Apache."

"Or for a white man, either," Chance said.

Lone Wolf looked at him closely, perhaps to see if Chance was mocking him. Satisfied, he nodded. "Or for a white man."

"If you tell the General, he can make things better."

"He tried. But he can't do enough. He is supposed to make certain the rules are not broken. He can't change the rules."

"But he can try."

Lone Wolf nodded. "Maybe yes. But not yet. First, the others have to come back. And the white man has to stop selling whiskey."

"If you tell me who it is, maybe I can do something."

"Maybe. Not yet."

With that, Lone Wolf turned and walked away. He didn't look back, even when Chance called after him. He was getting up to go after the Apache when Walker barged through the door behind him. "Who you talkin' to, Dalton? Looks like nobody's here. Maybe you been in the sun too long. I told you, you should come in."

Chance debated whether to tell Walker about his conversation, but decided to hold off for awhile. Then, with an ironic smile, he understood Lone Wolf's reluctance. Some things had to be shared cautiously. And some couldn't be shared at all. This one required caution.

Chance looked distracted, turned to Walker with a puzzled look on his face. "You say something, Tom?" he asked.

Walker grunted. "Let's git on home, unless there's anything you got to do while we're here."

"No, nothing."

"Alright, then. I guess Jenny'll be getting worried long about now."

"Martha, too," Chance said.

"Hell, no. The only thing Martha worries about is whether or not her garden's gonna grow this year. Once she knows the answer to that, she won't worry about nothing at all."

"You're overstating, as usual, Tom."

"Just a little." He clapped Chance on the shoulder, laughed once, and headed for his horse. Walker draped the bolt of calico over his shoulder, like a sentry on post, and did a stiff-legged strut. Chance laughed in spite of himself.

"Thank God the army's a little smoother than that, Tom. You wouldn't last a week under General Crook."

"The old geezer's really something, ain't he?" Walker said, as Chance caught up to him. "I wish to Christ he wasn't so damned concerned about bruising redskin feelings, though. I got a funny feeling about all this, Dalton. And I don't like it one damn bit."

"He knows what he's doing, Tom. You got to let him do what he thinks best."

"If you say so." Walker used rawhide thongs to tie the bolt of cloth over his saddle, like a bedroll. The red and white peeked out of either end of the brown paper, an incongruous dash of

color against the overwhelmingly dark tones of
Fort Apache.

When Chance climbed into his own saddle, he
glanced toward the Base Commander's office.
Lone Wolf was nowhere in sight, and the fort
looked even more deserted than when they'd arrived.

Walker wheeled his mount, and Chance followed suit. In ten minutes, he was able to look
back over his shoulder and watch the buildings re-
cede through the late afternoon shimmer. A thin
haze hung over the buildings, blurring everything
on the horizon and washing out the deep blues and
bright reds until they were little more than pastel
memories.

Walker slowed and nudged his horse in closer to
Chance. "What'd that Indian want? You ready to
tell me, yet?"

Chance shook his head. "Nothing, really."

"Dalton, don't be holding out on me, now. If he
told you something, I got to know about it. Too
much riding on this for you to be keeping secrets."

"Said he thought the Apaches had a beef. Said
he thought some had left the reservation, but it
wasn't official, and he didn't know for sure how
many we're talking about."

"Did he give you a rough idea?"

"Many. That's all he said. But I don't know if
that means five or fifty."

"More like fifty, to me," Walker said.

"Maybe so, Tom. But I got to think the General would know about fifty. Five or ten, maybe not. At least not right away. Hell, there's near twenty thousand on the reservation. A dozen is a drop in the bucket."

"You think so, Dalton?"

"Yeah, I do."

"Drop by later. I'll put a drop of cyanide in a bucket of water. You can drink all you want. How's that sound?"

"You're thinking like a lawman, Tom."

"That's what I am, Dalton. That's the way I'm paid to think."

He had a point.

8

THEY WERE ALMOST HOME as the sun began to set. They had been pushing their horses. Both men were anxious, and neither wanted to admit it. Instead, they took turns setting the pace. Chance had the feeling they were being watched, but he kept putting it aside. He told himself it was just a reaction to the past couple of days and, especially, to the information Lone Wolf had given him.

Knowing the Apaches were out there, it was hard to push it aside. He kept wondering whether he should tell Walker all of it. He wanted to, but something kept holding him back. Walker was a good man. He had no reservations on that score. He told him many bucks had broken out, but he didn't tell him Lone Wolf categorized them as bad ones. Maybe Walker ought to know. But there was a kind of hysteria in the air, and he didn't want to

feed it by getting the Sheriff on edge. The man had
enough to worry about.

As they approached the last leg, the sky turned
blue-black. A thin line of fire, almost like a crack
between earth and sky, traced the edges of the
mountains to the west. It was a brilliant white, and
Chance fancied he was watching light spill through
from someplace beyond the heavens. He slowed to
watch it, knowing that in a matter of minutes the
sky would be pitch black, and stay that way until
the moon came up.

It was getting cold, despite the torrid sun of the
afternoon. There was little to hold the heat, and
Chance wished he had brought a heavier coat.
Suppressing a shiver, he turned to Walker. "What
are you going to tell Jasper Green, Tom?"

"Hell, I don't know. Depends, I guess."

"On what?"

"On whether you're going to tell me everything
that redskin told you, or not."

"You back to that again?"

"Hell, yes, I'm back to that again. You owe it to
the folks in Cotton Springs to tell them whatever
you know, Dalton. They got families. Lives could
be at stake, here. If you know anything that can reassure them, you better tell me. And if you know
something they ought to be scared about, you
damn sure *better* tell me."

"Tom, it wasn't anything."

"Why not let me decide that?"

Chance didn't have an answer. Walker was right. But telling him what Lone Wolf had to say wouldn't change things. He sighed.

"Alright, Tom. You win."

"Course I do. I'm the Sheriff." He laughed, but it had a hollow ring to it.

Wayzata Canyon was just ahead. They had to go through it, or run an extra three miles. Neither choice was calculated to make them feel too secure. Chance looked at the yawning black mouth of the narrow canyon and shrugged his shoulders.

"I'm waiting, Dalton. I got all night, if you have."

"He said a few bucks had left the reservation. That Crook didn't know about it yet. But that he was looking into it."

"You already told me that much. What else did he say? He say who they were?"

"Not exactly, no."

"Damn it, Dalton, don't split hairs on me. Who? Geronimo one of them?"

"No. No names. Bad ones, that's all he said."

"Bad ones? And Crook don't know about it?"

"Nope. But he will."

"What makes you so sure?"

"Because Lone Wolf said he was going to find out exactly and tell him as soon as he was sure. I think that's what he said. That's what he meant, anyhow."

"Why didn't you tell Crook yourself, damn it?"

"Because I didn't want to go making a fuss. Now leave it alone, Tom. I told you what I know."

"Making a fuss? Is that what you said? You ever see a man split open from jawbone to gizzard, Dalton? You ever see a woman tore up so bad her own children couldn't recognize her, and wouldn't want to if they could? You ever see something like that?"

"I was in the cavalry for five years, Tom."

"Damn it, Dalton, that's no answer. Have you ever seen anything like that? I want to know, because if you haven't, then you don't know shit about a fuss."

Chance closed his eyes. He'd seen it, and worse. But he didn't want to think about it. Not now. Not when Jenny was alone with the kids, and he had nearly eight miles to go. "Yeah," he said. "Yeah, Tom, I have. Now leave me be."

Walker kicked his horse. He was madder than hell, and Chance figured he had a right to be. Walker barrelled for the mouth of the canyon, and Chance had to dig his spurs in to get his own horse moving. Walker was already pulling away, little more than a blur now, as the darkness of the canyon mouth swallowed him whole.

Chance pushed his mount even harder, but Walker kept the gap wide open. They were halfway through, or Chance was, when he heard the noise. A landslide, it sounded like. A sharp crack and a slow, rumbling thunder from somewhere up ahead. "Wait up, Tom," he shouted, but the noise was already too loud for Walker to hear him.

He rushed through the canyon at breakneck speed, hoping Walker had made it through the slide, or had enough warning to pull up. In the darkness, it was next to impossible to gauge just how far ahead the slide might be. The ground seemed to shake, when something, probably a huge slab of the red sandstone, hit the floor of the canyon. Smaller rocks were still falling, clattering with the hollow sound of old bones, when he rode into a choking cloud of dust. It was too thick for him to continue, and he jerked the reins sharply.

A few stray rocks continued to fall, and he remembered newspaper accounts of one of the old campaigns against Mangas Coloradas. The fearsome Apache chief had boasted of using rocks to kill enemies because "Mexicans weren't worth the bullets" it would take to kill them. Mangas was long since in the ground, but the technique was a good one.

"Tom?" Chance called. "Tom, you alright?"

"Over here," Walker called. "Chance, you hear me?"

"I'm coming. You alright?"

Walker shouted something else, but it was drowned out by a skitter of small stones rattling down the canyon wall and clattering across the ground. Sparks flew from the constant crack of stone on stone, little points of light, their brilliance muted by the heavy dust.

Chance had to struggle to control his mount. The frightened animal didn't want to move, and he had to be forced to angle away from the rock slide. Chance wrestled with him, using the bit and his spurs, and the horse began to respond.

A gun cracked, then again. The sharp report echoed off the canyon walls, and Chance couldn't tell where it came from.

"Tom?" he shouted. He heard his voice almost crack. He called again, and this time just his own voice came back, the words gone, leaving the empty hulls like hollow handclaps bouncing off the walls and coming back at him from every side. Again and again, slowly fading, as he repeated the call.

The Sheriff didn't answer him. Another gunshot, but this time he saw the muzzle flash. The bullet sailed just past his left ear and he fell out of the saddle. Landing on his right shoulder, he felt a stab of pain run down his side and explode in his hip.

His horse bolted before he could snag the reins. He tried to get up and run after it, but the animal was frightened. There was no way to catch it until it decided to stop on its own. And as he knelt there, it dawned on him that his Winchester had gone with his mount.

Groping for his gunbelt, he counted the bullets, found more empty loops than full ones. With six in his Colt's cylinder, he had maybe two dozen shells, probably fewer. Then, reaching for the Colt itself, he realized it was gone. He panicked. With a curse, he started to pat the ground all around him, his hands moving faster and faster, until his fingers closed over the barrel.

He hugged the pistol to his chest for a moment, suppressed the urge to kiss the cold metal. Then he started to crawl. He heard voices, but they were too far away for him to tell what they were saying. He couldn't even determine the language.

Chance found a rock and leaned against it, waiting for the pain in his side to diminish. He had to find some way to get to Walker, but he had to think. There was no point in getting himself shot, too.

Lying there, trying to piece it together, he wondered why Apaches would have been waiting in the canyon after dark. Like most Indians, they fought at night only when they had to. Nobody had to fight him and Walker. No way they could have been surprised, because a deaf man could have heard Walker's horse a quarter mile away. It was almost like a deliberate ambush, like they had been waiting there on purpose.

But why?

He almost asked the question aloud. And there was no answer that made any sense. Gritting his teeth, he pushed it aside. He got to his feet. His hip felt a little better, and his shoulder throbbed, but nothing seemed to be broken. He would live, he knew that.

Unless whoever was out there was looking for him. If it was an ambush, did they know there would be two men? He couldn't answer that, but decided he better act like the answer was yes. Chance started through the thinning dust, trying to muffle his footsteps, and moving away from the wall of the canyon until he was almost dead center. It was too dark to see more than a few feet ahead now, and Walker had to be a damn fool to come charging in here like he did. Then, remembering their conversation, he realized Tom had been running for home to make sure the word got out as soon as possible. He had been doing his job, and damn the cost.

The voices had stopped now, and he strained to hear anything at all in the pitch black hole. Except for the creak and groan of rocks still shifting, there was nothing.

Then a horse whinnied, and a second. The squeak of leather was followed by hoofbeats.

Chance started toward the sound, but couldn't make much headway in the darkness. He stopped to listen. It sounded like the horses were shod. He heard the distinct click of metal on stone. Were they Apaches on stolen horses?

Or were they white men?

He heard the snuffling sound of another horse. It was close. Chance dropped to the ground and listened. His eyes fighting the cloud of sifting dust. There, he heard it again.

A hoof pawing the ground now, almost on top of him, and then, looming up out of the dust, was Walker's horse. He reached for the reins and snagged them on the second try.

When he stood up, the frightened animal started to run, and Chance had all he could do to drag it to a standstill, digging in his heels and putting all his weight on the reins. Fighting the bit, the animal shook its head, trying to break loose.

Moving in close, Chance patted the animal's neck. It was still damp with sweat. Moving to the other side, he groped for the boot, found Walker's carbine, and slipped it out, trying to make no noise.

Covering the safety with his palm, he clicked it off. Holding his breath, he worked the lever. It clicked sharply, but it couldn't be helped. With a round in the chamber, he leaned forward, holding the Winchester out in front of him and curving his body almost protectively around the butt.

It took him almost an hour to find Walker.

And he knew, before he knelt down, that he was an hour too late.

9

THEY HAD BEEN TOO NERVOUS to talk about it. Waiting all afternoon, drinking a little, then a little more, they sat quietly. An occasional chair would scrape the rough wooden floor as one or another of them got up to go outside and relieve himself in the bushes. He'd come back, pour himself another drink and look at the others.

Some of them were less frightened than confused. None of them was happy. Eight men with one secret, and not one of them wanted to be the first to say he objected. Instead, each of them sat there, trying to drown his discomfort in whatever came to hand, watered whiskey, beer, even plain old water. But nothing worked. After every drink, the job was still there staring them all in the face. The rags, cut burlap, really, and the ball of rough twine sat like a monument to what they were about to do. Looking at it, they couldn't help but remember.

Once, one of the men stood up, gathered the rags and twine into his arms and carried them to a corner of the room. He stopped for a moment in front of the fireplace, where a small fire, just enough to heat a pot of coffee, continued to chew at the pair of logs propped over a third, thicker one. The room smelled of wood-smoke and stank of sweat.

Outside, the sun was starting to sink. It would be dark in a little more than an hour. Before then they would have to decide whether they were in or out. It would be the last opportunity to say no. And each man, as he drank, looked at the others, trying to decide who among them all would be the first to say no. Or would any of them.

The night couldn't come soon enough. They all wanted the night to come, some because it meant the morning would come soon after, and some because they were anxious to get to work. They were well paid, and they did what they were told to do. That's how they earned their money. But this new scheme seemed crazy. No way it could work. It just couldn't.

But the boss said do it.

And they would do it, because they wanted to keep on working. And they wanted to keep on making good money. Occasionally a horse would whinny, and one of the men would get up and walk to the window. The rumors about the Apaches were getting more frequent. Most of them had been here long enough to know what that could mean, if the stories were true.

"I guess it's about time, boys," one of them said. He was almost indistinguishable from the others, who all looked enough like one another to be cousins, at least, members of an extended family. They had been shaped by their years on the edge of the high desert, by years of fighting everything from Arapahos to Yankees, and most of all, each other. The conflict had worn the edges away, much the way the constant current will grind each pebble into a rough approximation of all the others.

There was no room for differences, let alone differences of opinion. They were white men, and they had to stick together. That was the only rule.

Or so they told themselves.

The one who spoke stood up. He teetered a little unsteadily, but the others didn't notice. Leaning over slightly to balance himself on the edge of the table, he waited for somebody to answer him, or to argue with him, but none did. Instead, one by one, they all stood up. Then, crowding toward the door with a jangle of spurs, they filed outside. Their horses were already saddled. The last man out looked at the string and burlap, gathered it in his arms and pulled the cabin door closed behind him.

Taking time to stuff the burlap into his saddle-bags, he was the last to climb into the saddle. He realized it and wondered whether he was the most reluctant. Deciding there was no way to know, he shrugged. The first horses had already begun to move. He dug the rowels into his own mount's flanks and brought up the rear.

It was a ten mile ride, and during it, no one said a word. The hooves of the mounts thudded on the dry ground, and saddle leather squeaked. An occasional spur jingled. The rest was the silence of the night. A martin or a bat flashed overhead, then the sky was empty. The moon wasn't up yet, and the landscape was a mass of shadows.

The man in the lead kept glancing back, as if to make sure the others hadn't deserted him. The rider in the drag position kept hoping, if he slowed enough, their momentum would run out. He could slow them, they would come to a halt, change their minds and ride away, forget about all this bullshit.

But underneath it all, the resentment, simmering like a stew on a low flame, bubbled. The hatred, never really very far from the surface, didn't take much to uncover it. Some of it was understandable, maybe even justified. They had all lost someone in the family to the life out here, most to Indians, and somebody might as well pay for it. Getting paid to get even was a rare opportunity. How could they afford not to take advantage of it?

But it was all lies, a way to justify what they were about to do. They knew it, and they were ready to do it anyway.

When they reached the rise overlooking a small bowl of a valley, the moon had come up. The camp, edged back under the shadow of the mesa, was quiet. They had time yet, but not much.

The rancheria was small, no more than ten or twelve wickiups. Under the high desert moon, which spilled pale light like clear water over the cottonwoods beneath the looming rock, the huts sat still as boulders. In the center, the remains of a pair of campfires still glowed dully. When the cool night breeze swirled through the camp, small puffs of ashes rose, winking like fireflies. The beds of coals turned from deep red to yellow-orange for a few moments, then died back to the darker color. Small clouds of smoke rose a few inches, then were torn apart and disappeared.

High on another mesa to the southwest, a coyote, its forepaws propped on a slab of stone, was outlined against the dark blue of the sky. One side was painted silver by the moon. He barked, then yipped, challenging the night, but soon lost interest, dropped to the table top of the mesa, and disappeared.

The eight men huddled in a second stand of cottonwoods, watching the campsite. None of them spoke. The time passed slowly for them, and they tried to keep still, fearful some accidental noise might alarm the Indians.

They waited for more than two hours, their courage inflamed by whiskey, but not enough yet to move out into the open. With every hiss of the wind through the sun-stiffened leaves, they looked around, guilty as school boys playing hookie. To help pass the time, they had painted their faces, smearing them with a paste of river mud and cold ashes, blackening their cheeks like minstrels, leaving nothing but the rolling whites of nervous eyes visible among the trees. They couldn't recognize each other anymore, and that made them all feel a little better.

Their boots were wrapped in the burlap rags, now tied around their ankles with the cheap twine. The coyote called again, this time from the far side of the mesa. The bone-chilling sound made one of the men shudder.

"I ain't too sure I like this," he whispered. He wasn't addressing anyone in particular. The other men knew it. No one bothered to answer him. He started to back up, snapping a twig, and one of his companions grabbed him by the arm.

"You wanta get us all killed, you fool?" He whispered, too, and the harsh rasp cut through the silence. To cover their own nervousness, the others glared at the two men. It gave them something to be mad at, and that made them a little less afraid. But not much.

The man who whispered let go of the man who backed up, then wiped his sweaty palms on his shirt. Right away, he felt new moisture, but he was not about to back down. Not now. Not this close.

"Been a long time since anybody moved over there," he whispered.

"Let's get it over with, then," one of the others said.

The man who had backed up said, "Maybe we should wait a bit more."

"Hell, we can wait all night, Roy. Maybe we can hang around till breakfast. That suit you alright?"

"Bastard," Roy said.

He stepped through the last line of trees, brushing the branches aside with one arm. His hands felt slick on the stock of his Winchester, and he kept shifting the carbine from hand to hand, alternately wiping his palms on the legs of his dungarees. The grit of the high desert sand dried them for a moment. For some reason, he found it interesting, almost stopping to look, and tilting one hand to try to catch the moonlight on his hand, to see if it really was dry.

The others moved past him, walking on tip-toe, the rags muffling the sound of their footsteps, and leaving strange, rounded impressions in the layer of dust coating the dry ground. At the first wickiup, the lead man stopped. He shook his head once, then waved a stout stick wrapped with a coarse rag soaked in coal oil. When the others joined him, he tip-toed into the center of the rancheria, brandishing the stick like a club until he got close enough to poke it into the ashes of the nearest campfire.

The coal oil caught, sending a thin string of black smoke wiggling up as if to get away from the sudden balloon of light as the makeshift torch burst into flame.

A second torch was lit as another man joined him. Moving more quickly now, almost forgetting to stay on tip-toe, they moved from wickiup to wickiup, splashing more coal oil on the stiff hide walls. The last one doused was the first one torched.

When flames had begun to slaver up the walls of all twelve, they backed away and waited. It wouldn't be long.

Arranged in a half circle, just outside the perimeter of the camp, the eight men fiddled with the triggers on their rifles. Someone either smelled smoke or heard the crackle of the flames, because a sudden shout pierced the night. Other shouts answered, confused, and frightened. A moment later, people began spilling out of the lodges.

The men began shooting.

It was easy to find their targets, outlined by the harsh orange light, as they scurried in aimless circles. People began to slap at the buildings with blankets, trying to put out the flames, almost oblivious to the shooting, as if they couldn't hear it, or as if they couldn't believe it was happening and therefore there was no reason to pay any attention to the sound of the gunfire.

Slowly, it seemed to dawn on the Indians. They started running for the trees. Methodically, the shooters picked them off until they had run so far into the shadows that the light no longer reached them.

The methodical brutality of it seemed to stun them all at once. They backed away, as if repelled by the realization of what they had done.

They were back in the saddle before Roy said, "How come they didn't shoot back?"

No one answered him.

10

CHANCE WATCHED THE MOON RISE, slowly filling Wayzata Canyon with silver light and blue gray shadows. He sat a few feet from Tom Walker's body, with the reins of Walker's horse tangled in one fist. The sound of the night kept his nerves on edge, and he kept his Colt in his lap, stroking it idly with curled fingers.

He didn't want to think about the morning, especially not that part of it that would take him to see Martha Walker. Part of him hoped the sun would never rise again. But then he would think of Jenny and the boys. She was a strong woman, but she must be frantic by now. And his family were the only ones who knew he was missing.

Come morning, Jimmy Slattery would realize the Sheriff hadn't made it home, and he'd mount a search. But that was hours away. Reluctantly,

Chance got to his feet, looked at Walker once more, and shook his head. Untangling the reins from his fist, he swung into the saddle and nudged the horse back toward the mouth of the canyon. He'd need his own mount, and hoped it wouldn't be impossible to find.

The moon was behind him, just above the rim-rock, and spilled his shadow forward. Distorted by the angle of the light, it looked like an ink stain on gray paper. It bobbed and changed shape as he moved, and he didn't want to look at it.

It took him an hour to recapture his own horse, and when he got back to Walker's body, the moon had already started to set. Dismounting, he tied both horses to a scrub oak, stunted by the lack of light in the deep ravine, and struggled to hoist Tom Walker onto his horse, draping him over the saddle after two failed attempts.

He cut a short length of rope to hold the corpse in place, untied Walker's horse, then his own. Back in the saddle, he laced Walker's reins to his own saddle and urged his horse on toward Cotton Springs.

By the time he reached the end of the canyon, the sun was already beginning to rise. A flattened arc of bright red crept above the edge of the mountains to his left, and he watched a few rags of clouds turn from purple to pink and finally to blue-white.

The horses seemed subdued, as if they were exhausted, which was probable, or aware in some strange way of what had happened, which Chance knew was unlikely. But it seemed fitting somehow to think it.

He hit the road into town a little over an hour later. The weathered sign, listing the population as two hundred and eleven was almost unreadable. And it hadn't been accurate in years. People came and went, and nobody bothered to count anymore. Whenever a baby was born, or somebody got planted, the story went, Deke Joseph used to come out and paint over the old number, then paint the new one in. But it soon reached a point where the valley started to fill, and nobody was sure whether a spread in the valley made one a citizen of the town, or not.

Fed up with the constant bickering, Deke had stopped painting the sign, and folks pretty much stopped giving a damn, one way or another. Riding past the sun-splintered wood, Chance shook his head. Deke would have his work cut out in the next few weeks, if the past couple of days were any indication. Chance thought it just as well nobody bothered anymore.

He headed straight for the Sheriff's office. As he entered the main street, he looked back once, but quickly turned away. Seeing Tom Walker hanging over his horse like that made him want to cry. He pushed the feeling away, chewed his lower lip and straightened his back just a little.

The front door of the office was open when he reined in. He heard footsteps from inside as he slid down from the saddle. Jimmy Slattery was in the doorway, a puzzled look on his face. "Christ Almighty, Dalton," he said, "what you got there?"

Then he recognized the horse.

"Oh, my God. That's Tom, ain't it?" One hand went to his mouth, and he chewed his knuckles for a second, one foot suspended in mid stride. Regaining his composure, he jumped down to the hard-packed dirt and moved toward the horse, slowing up as he did so, until the last couple of yards seemed as if they would never end.

"Jeezus, what happened?"

Chance told him.

Slattery was wringing his hands now, looking from Walker's body to Chance and back. "How in the hell am I gonna tell Martha? How in the hell can I do that, Dalton? I can't do that . . . I can't tell her that. Jeezus."

"You better run and see if Zack Morely is open. We're gonna need him."

"Zack's open. Sure, Zack's always open. I'll go get him." Glad for an excuse to get away from the hard truth staring him in the face, Slattery was already moving. Chance watched him go, walking faster and faster, then breaking into a run. Up the street, he spotted a couple of shopkeepers, and Red Malone was on his porch, drying his hands on his apron.

Chance watched the bartender run into the street to intercept Slattery. The deputy slowed down, turning to finish telling Malone as he moved on past. Malone broke into a trot. The other shopkeepers ran after him.

Chance stood there watching them race toward him, the reins trailing away from his hand. Malone, out of breath, was the first to reach him.

"Dalton," he said, then stopped. "Jaysus, it really is Tom isn't it? I thought maybe I misheard Slats. You alright?"

Chance nodded. "I guess."

"What happened?"

"Red, listen, I don't want to keep tellin' it over and over. Wait'll later. Slattery will get the mayor and the other deputies. I'll tell it once. Then I don't think I want to talk about it anymore."

Malone nodded. "Sure, Dalton. Sure enough, boyo. Why don't you go on inside? You look like hell."

Chance handed the reins to Malone, tied off his own mount, and walked heavily to the open front door. Inside, he sat on a wooden bench facing Tom Walker's desk. He looked around the small room, already beginning to heat up from the morning sun. He'd been here so many times, but had never

looked at it so closely before. It seemed so small a
place for a man to spend his whole life, especially
when there was so much room out there, just past
the edge of town. So cramped, it made him feel like
he was suffocating.

He heard the sounds of a small crowd gathering,
and tried to blot it out. He knew what was coming, but he didn't want to think about it. Already
the voices were getting angry. He heard the word
Apache at least a dozen times. And he knew there
was no way those angry men outside were going to
hear him when he said he wasn't sure. They already knew what they wanted to believe, and they
would hear it whether he told them so or not.

Boots scraped on the wooden walk, and the
light in the doorway beside him grew dim. He
looked up into the beard and scowling face of
Warren Montrose, the town's mayor, and the
biggest landowner in the valley.

Montrose sighed, then scraped across the floor
and dropped into Walker's chair. "Chance, you
mighty lucky to get home."

"I know it."

"You want to tell me what happened?"

"No, but I guess I got to."

"Not tellin' it won't change nothing, Dalton.
You know that."

"Yeah, Warren, I know. I do know it. But I keep
thinking maybe . . ."

"Apaches, wasn't it? Jasper Green was right. That old fussbudget must have cried wolf a thousand times since he come to Cotton Springs. But I reckon this one time he was right."

"I don't know about that, Warren."

"Course you do, Dalton. Had to be. Who else woulda done it? Back shot him, too, looks like."

"You're not listening to me, Warren. I said I don't know for sure if it was Apaches or not. There was a rock slide in Wayzata Canyon. I didn't see what happened. Only heard the shots and heard horses. I'm pretty sure the horses were shod. Apaches don't do that."

"Course they don't. That's why they steal ours, Dalton. Let us put the shoes on for 'em."

"You know of any horses been stolen lately?"

"Not right now, I don't. But I reckon if we ask around, we'll find out soon enough."

"We ask around after what happened, you can bet your ass somebody'll say so, but that won't prove anything."

"We got all the proof we need, Dalton, right outside hangin' over Tommy Walker's saddle. If that ain't proof enough for you, then I don't know what is."

"Warren, I . . ."

But Montrose cut him off. The mayor had already made up his mind, just as Chance had known he would. Nobody wanted any doubts.

Nobody wanted to think that maybe there was some other explanation. And at the moment, Dalton Chance didn't give a damn. He was tired and he wanted to go home. He started to get up.

"Where you goin', Dalton?"

"Thought I'd ride over to Tom's place. Somebody's got to tell Martha."

"I can handle that. Why don't you go on home and see to Jenny and the boys. I'll come by later and we can talk some more, after you get some rest."

"You sure?"

"Hell, yes, I'm sure. I've known Martha for a dozen years. She might as well hear it from me, if she has to hear it from anybody."

Montrose stood up and walked toward the door. He clapped Dalton on the shoulder. "Hell, son, we'll fix those murderin' bastards, don't you worry none about that."

"I think I should worry, Warren. People go off half-cocked, somebody who don't deserve it's gonna get hurt."

"You let me worry about that. 'Sides, I never yet met an Apache, heard of one either, didn't deserve hangin'. Nobody else is gonna get hurt, so you can just put your mind at ease on that score."

Chance shook his head. He didn't want to argue. Maybe after the first rush of passion was behind him, Montrose would be ready to listen to reason. Then again, maybe Apaches *did* do it. Chance's problem was he just didn't know. Being uncertain, he had practically no chance at all to convince the people of Cotton Springs to keep an open mind. Maybe the best thing to do was just to go on home and worry about the ones who mattered most. The rest would sort itself out.

11

AS CHANCE CAME OVER THE HILL, Jenny was on the front porch. She was sitting in a rocker, but the chair was motionless. It looked for a moment as if she had been turned into something like Lot's Wife, frozen in time to sit there forever on the verge of movement, but never quite breaking free of the stasis.

Then she saw Chance. She was out of the chair and running. Her hair, still undone from the night before, flew out behind her like the tail of a coal-black comet. He was off the horse in an instant, caught her in his arms and lifted her off the ground.

"Damn you, Dalton. I was so worried." She buried her face in the hollow beneath his jaw as he spun her around. She squeezed so hard, he felt as if his ribs might crack. The tender place on his shoulder sent a spurt of flame down his side, but he didn't give a damn.

"Where are the boys?" he asked, lowering her to the ground.

"Sleeping. They were up half the night. They wanted to keep me company, but it was just too much for them. They fell asleep just before dawn."

She realized then that something was wrong. Backing away a step or two, she raised one fist to the corner of her mouth. "What's happened?" Her voice trembled, but didn't quite break.

"Tom Walker's dead," he said. "Shot dead, over in Wayzata Canyon. I . . ." He stopped, not knowing how to go on.

"Does Martha know?"

He thought that was just like her. To see immediately what mattered most. "Warren Montrose is riding out to Tom's place."

"You should have gone with him. The man's a lout. He doesn't know how to handle this sort of thing."

"I know I should have, but . . . I just wanted to come home. I was worried, and I guess I didn't really know how to tell Martha anyway. I knew I'd make it worse than it had to be."

"Not you, Dalton. That's Warren. That's what he'll do."

"He's not that bad, Jen."

"Yes. He is that bad, Dalton. At something like this, anyway."

"There's no good way to tell it, Jen. You know that."

"Still . . ."

"I want to see the boys." He draped an arm around her shoulder and half pulled her toward the house.

"Don't wake them, Dalton."

"I won't. I just want to see them, that's all. Make sure they're alright."

He stepped onto the porch and opened the front door quietly. He couldn't help but notice the shotgun leaning against the wall behind the rocking chair. He didn't mention it.

Tip-toeing toward the boys' room, he tried not to jangle his spurs. The boys were both light sleepers, especially Curt, and once they were up, they stayed up. He wanted a little time to himself with Jenny. But he had to see them first.

He walked to the foot of the bed and stood looking down. Dalton Jr. opened one eye. He seemed confused for a second, then, recognizing Dalton, he smiled. He was asleep again a second later. Moving around the side of the bed, he reached out and brushed a lock of hair away from Curt's brow. Looking at Jenny, he mouthed the words, "He needs a haircut."

"Later," she mimed. And he nodded. Later

would be fine, now that he was certain there would *be* a later.

He backed away from the bed, unwilling to turn and take his eyes off his sons. At the doorway, he paused, conscious of Jenny hovering just behind him. She put a hand on his shoulder, tugged him away, and pushed him toward their bedroom. She closed the door to the boys' room, then whispered, "Dalton, get some sleep, honey. You need to rest."

"Come with me," he said.

He entered their bedroom and lay down on the bed without bothering to take off his boots. She sat beside him for a moment, and he took a handful of her hair. "So soft," he said and fell asleep.

Jenny pulled a light blanket up over him, not wanting him to lie uncovered, but knowing it was going to be unbearably hot in another hour. She backed out of the room, closed the door and went to the kitchen. Sitting at the table, she buried her face in her hands. But there was no point now. Dalton was home, and everything was going to be alright. She wanted to know what had happened, but she knew, too, that knowing might be worse than not knowing. For now, it was enough to know that Tom Walker was dead. And that Martha probably knew. And that there was nothing anybody could do to change what Martha knew.

The sound on the front porch, a slight creak, almost escaped her attention. She listened for a second, then remembered the shotgun. Where was it? As it came to her, she stood up and saw a shadow fall across the doorway.

She froze for a second. The shadow grew darker, then filled the doorway. Jenny screamed without realizing it. The man in the doorway looked at her, a finger to his lips. She screamed again. She heard Dalton call her, then the sound of the door opening.

"Dalton," she shouted, "Dalton . . ."

He came through the doorway just as the front door opened. He saw the Indian at the same instant. He reached for his gun, but the Indian raised his hands.

"I am sorry," Lone Wolf said.

Chance put his arms around his wife. "It's alright, Jenny. It's alright. I know him. It's alright." Jenny began to sob, waking the boys. They called to her, and Chance hushed her. "Jenny, it's alright. Go tell the boys it's alright."

He watched her go, not turning to Lone Wolf until she had disappeared through the doorway. Lone Wolf gestured to Chance to follow him outside.

Chance closed the front door behind him and sat on the porch. The Apache stood on the ground, his back to the house. "I found out what you wanted to know," he said.

"How many?"

"Fifteen."

"Does General Crook know?"

"I told him, yes."

"Bad ones?"

Lone Wolf didn't answer right away. He turned to face Chance. "All Apaches are alike, aren't they?"

"I don't think so, no. All white men aren't alike. Why should Apaches be any different?"

The Apache nodded. It seemed to confirm an expectation for him. But he didn't elaborate. Instead, he said, "Bad ones, yes. Very bad."

"The General will take care of it?"

"When he can, yes. But the Army takes much time. Supplies have to be packed. Two, maybe three days before anything will happen."

"Too long?"

"Too long, yes. After last night."

"You know about last night?"

The Apache seemed surprised. "I didn't know that you knew."

"Was it Apaches?"

Lone Wolf looked puzzled. "No, of course not. Why would you think that?"

"That's what folks around here think. I'm not sure, and I'm the only one who was there."

"You were there?" Again, Lone Wolf seemed confused.

Chance noticed. "We are talking about the same thing, aren't we? The Sheriff?"

"The Sheriff?"

"Yes, the man who was with me yesterday. At the fort. He was killed last night. On the way home. That's what we're talking about, isn't it?"

"No. I was talking about the village on the Santa Rita. The attack on the rancheria."

"Attack? On a village?"

"Many dead. Twenty seven. Women. Old men. Children."

"You mean the renegades attacked their own people? Children? I don't believe it."

"Not the renegades, no. White men. I know this. I saw the rancheria this morning. What is this about the Sheriff?"

Chance told him. Lone Wolf seemed almost not to be listening. When he was finished, he watched the Apache carefully, wondering whether Lone Wolf knew more than he seemed to.

"Show me the place where it happened."

"Why?"

"To know. To see whether it was as you think it was."

"You mean whether white men did it? Is that what you mean?"

"Not just white men. Maybe the same white men. The ones who attacked the village."

"How could you tell that?"

Lone Wolf didn't answer. There was no need. Chance knew very well that Lone Wolf was a member of a tribe that could cover a hundred miles a day, across high desert. One that knew every square inch of the land from the Colorado border all the way to the heart of the Sierra Madres. They could follow a man where no one else could see a sign of his passing. It was how they were raised. And it was, more than that, how they survived.

Shrugging to avoid the obvious, Chance asked, "What difference would it make? It won't bring Tom back. Or your people, either."

"But if the same men did both things, then maybe it makes a difference. There is a reason. Maybe."

"What reason? How could there be a reason to shoot a man in the back?"

"What reason could there be to shoot a child in the back? Do white men have a reason for such things? Apaches don't."

Chance didn't know how to answer the question. "Of course not, no. There is no reason for that, either. I only meant that whatever had happened has happened. We can't change it, not you and not me."

"But maybe we can change what will happen.

Maybe not you or me. But maybe you and me. Maybe we can do that."

Chance knew what the Apache was saying. But he didn't want to think about it. If he didn't ask questions, he wouldn't know the answers. And if he didn't know the answers, then he would be left alone. He was out of it, and he wanted to stay out of it.

"Look," he said, "I'm sorry. This is something for General Crook. If you know anything, anything about who did it, tell the General. I can't do anything about it. Tell General Crook."

"I did tell him."

"And what does he say?"

"He says he needs proof. I will get it, but it will take time. The men who are selling the whiskey are the same men who attacked the village. And probably the same men who killed your Sheriff Walker."

"Look, I'd like to help, but . . ."

The Apache nodded. "I understand."

Chance shook his head. "It's not what you think. I mean, it's not because you're an Indian. That's not it. It's just, there's nothing I can do. Nothing that can make things different. The people here are angry, and they won't listen to me. And I don't really have anything to tell them, anyway."

"Suppose you did have something? Would that make a difference?"

"Not to them, no."

"To you?"

"I don't know. I'm sorry, but I just don't know."

The Apache nodded.

12

CHANCE SAT ON THE HILL. Far to the south, moving slowly, a small wagon train curved across the barren bottomland. The plume of dust it kicked up curled once then hung in the air, flattening out like the top of an anvil thunderhead. He threw the glasses on the lead wagon, then the second and finally the third.

To look at it, you would think it was no different from any other caravan, crossing the wasteland by the dozens on the way to California. But if the rumors were right, and Dalton Chance no longer doubted it, this one was anything but ordinary. The flat valley bottom was almost devoid of cover. It would be virtually impossible for him to get much closer without running the risk of being spotted.

And Chance couldn't afford that. If his suspi-

cions were right, the wagons were full of whiskey.
More than suspicions, really. Lone Wolf had told
him. He didn't want to hear it, but he was curious.
Somebody had to pay for Tom Walker. And it
seemed more than likely that whoever had killed
the Sheriff was also smuggling whiskey onto the
reservation. Lone Wolf had intimated even more,
and Jasper Green had named names. But Chance
wasn't willing to go that far. Not yet. Not without
proof. Not that he didn't believe the Apache or
Jasper. But no one else would. Jasper had a reputation. And the Apache was . . . well, an Apache.
So, he needed proof.

He didn't want to act rashly. He wanted certainty in an uncertain world. Suddenly, he had
sympathy for the caution of George Crook. One
had to be sure.

He had been following them for an hour and a
half, feeling guilty every mile. So far, he had seen
nothing odd, nothing suspicious. The wagons were
plain flatbeds with canvas drawn snug and laced
tightly over their lumpy freight.

Bringing the glasses to bear on the lead wagon
again, he watched the two men on the seat, one
talking a mile a minute, the other fussing with a
plug of chewing tobacco, nodding occasionally,
but mostly just listening. He had seen one of the
men, the driver, before, but couldn't place him.
That, too, would come to him if he were patient.

The wagons seemed to be drifting toward a huge column of red rock, jutting up off the valley floor like the chimney after the house is gone. A good place to rendezvous, he thought. A landmark like that would be impossible to miss. But was it a rendezvous or not? He wondered.

He thought about Lone Wolf, wishing the Apache were here with him, cursing himself for that stubborn pride and the even more stubborn desire for revenge that had terrorized his sleepless nights for more than two weeks. But it was too late to rebuild that particular bridge. He had burned it without thinking, and now he would have to pay the price. But if he was going to get enough evidence to satisfy Crook, then he was going to have to stick it out.

Shifting the glasses again to survey the base of the red chimney, he spotted another cloud of dust, this one much smaller, already half dispersed, as if it had been there for some time. Twiddling the focus knob on the binoculars, he tried to resolve the image swimming in the glass. But the super-heated air swirling up off the desert floor made everything look vague, as if it were melting in the intense heat.

Chance swore under his breath, then let the glasses fall. Shaking his head, he squeezed his chestnut just enough to urge it over the ridge at a slow walk. As he angled down the bone dry hill, the caravan started up a gentle rise. It would be out of sight in ten or fifteen minutes, and he could push his mount a little harder then, closing the gap a bit, until he rode up the same rise. Then he'd have to wait again.

That had been going on for two weeks. Hurry up, wait, hurry up. Wait.

And so far he didn't have a damn thing to show for it, not even a hint that Lone Wolf might be right. And in the back of his mind was the nagging suspicion that maybe the Apache had been trying to send him on a wild goose chase. Covering for his own kind, he extended a finger, expecting the gullible white man to follow where it pointed.

Well, he had taken the bait. The only question now was whether or not there was a fish. He glanced at the sun, checked his pocket watch, then looked back at the sun. It had started to sink, and he only had about two hours of daylight left. Once it got dark, he'd have to make sure he didn't ride right up their backs. That would be the easiest way to get himself killed. If Lone Wolf was right . . . he tried to dismiss it, tried to find a reason not to believe the Apache.

And he didn't doubt it anymore. Something had changed him. Maybe it was those nights staring at the ceiling, hearing the killers leaving the scene. Over and over again, those hooves. Shod hooves clicking on the stone.

And according to Slattery, no report of stolen horses. Word had reached Cotton Springs from Fort Apache. Fifteen bucks gone. But so far, not a sign. Nothing. Unless you believed they'd killed Tom Walker. That was something it seemed everyone but Chance did believe. But they believed because they wanted to, not because they had any way of knowing. The army position, officially, was that the renegades had gone to Mexico, to the Sierra Madres. But the people of Cotton Springs weren't so sure.

He felt guilty leaving Jenny alone this morning. But he didn't know what else to do. If the Apaches were innocent, then somebody had to prove it. And if they weren't, then the sooner they had proof, the sooner they would all be safe again. If he could look General Crook right in the eye and tell him, "Yes, I saw Tucker Wiley's men selling whiskey to Apaches . . ."

But he hadn't seen it. Not yet. And when the wagons had moved past earlier that day, he had debated whether or not to follow them. At first, he rejected the idea. But the more he thought about it, the more he knew he couldn't walk away from it. So, here he was, following three rollicking buckboards across the beautiful heart of hell, and so far he wasn't even close to having anything to show for it.

When the wagons broke the horizon then

started drifting down the far side of the hill, he nudged his horse over and down. He could push it now, make up some ground. They might see the dust trail his mount kicked up, but it wasn't a perfect world. He had to take a risk in order to win anything.

When he reached the first gentle swell of the next incline, he slowed his horse to a walk. Standing in the stirrups and looking across the valley floor behind him, he could see the trail the wagons had left, the hoofprints of his horse and the wagon mules, and a faint rooster comb of fine beige dust, pointing back the way he'd come.

He told himself it still wasn't too late to turn back. Nobody knew he'd come. It wasn't his business. Let the army handle it, when they got ready, and when there was proof they even had something to handle. All he wanted to do was lead his own life. Why the hell did he have to get involved?

But there was an easy answer to that question, and he couldn't lie to himself. He got involved precisely because it *was* his business. The minute anyone began to tamper with the delicate balance that was the only thing between the white man and the Apache, it was every man's business, white and red alike.

Again, he thought of Lone Wolf. The scout gave him the creeps. He was like some speaking stone, one that somehow knew things others didn't know, because he could go where others couldn't go. It was spooky, the way Lone Wolf looked at him with those black eyes glittering like marbles, like he saw things he didn't know how to describe, and hoped you would see for yourself. As if he believed that, by looking at him, you could see with him.

Chance dismounted. A stunted saguaro was the only thing available to tether his mount, and he looped the reins gingerly around the thick, waxy-looking trunk, trying to avoid the six-inch needles. Snatching his Winchester from its boot, he scrambled up the slope. He gripped the binoculars in one hand, the rifle in the other, and leaned forward to keep his balance on the loose dirt.

He dropped to the ground and crawled the last few yards. He hesitated only once, when the tell-tale squiggle of a recent sidewinder caught his eye. He brushed the track away, as if afraid the snake might follow it back to him, and finished his sprawling climb.

With the glasses, he swept the floor of the next valley. It was wide and shallow, more like a meat platter than a bowl. The uniformity of its light, reddish-brown soil was broken by stray saguaro here and there, but otherwise unrelieved. He could see the wagons clearly, but the approaching party was hidden by the torrid shimmer rising off the valley floor.

He moved the glasses to the base of the chimney

rock, trying to focus through the smeared base. It still looked as if both parties were converging on the chimney. It made sense. In a barren hell like this, you didn't want to miss your connection. The best way to guarantee you wouldn't was to pick a rendezvous only a blind man could miss.

The wagons turned in a wide, shallow arc, moving more slowly now, so that no dust was kicked up. A small cloud still trailed behind the approaching riders. The way it swelled and contracted made it look as if a huge, rusty ball were rolling across the high desert right behind them.

Chance wanted to get closer, but there was no place to hide. He would be wide open. If the meeting was illegal, as he was almost certain it had to be, the men would be cautious. Even out here in the middle of nowhere, wisdom, if not a guilty conscience, required care.

He wondered about the spare horses trailing behind the wagons. They were saddled, and well cared for. But why expose them to the heat? It didn't make sense. The oncoming riders veered off to the right now, heading right toward the wagons. He watched as the wagons slowly rolled to a halt. The men sat there. They were just barely in focus. They came in and out of clear sight as waves of heat rolled across the valley, distorting everything for a few seconds, then bringing it into sharp relief before blurring it again.

While he watched, he kept thinking about the horses. Then it came to him so suddenly, it was almost as if he had known it all along. They would leave the wagons, and ride back on their own horses. He should have realized it before now.

But what about payment? If it was whiskey in the wagons, what did the riders, presumably Apaches, have to pay for it? Wagons and riders were little more than five hundred yards apart now. There was no sign of panic from the wagons. Clearly they were expecting the other party.

Chance watched the riders exclusively now. The way they came and went, like mirages, made him furious. Slowly, an image would start to resolve. He'd see a flash of color, catch a glint of metal of some sort, then it would all distort, leaving him with nothing to fix his vision on.

Again and again, he came to the edge of certainty, only to see it slip away, melted by the hot desert sun. He was talking to himself now, urging the riders on, closer, close enough for him to see, once and for all, who they were.

Shifting back to the wagons, he was surprised to see the men untying the canvas covers. As he watched, they peeled back the covers, tugging them toward the front of each wagon. He couldn't see over the sides of the wagons, but he didn't have to. He already knew what was in them.

Back on the riders, this time he had better luck.

One man came into sudden, sharp focus, just for an instant, then melted away. But there was no mistaking it. The long black hair, the red headband and loose cotton shirt were incontrovertible. Apaches. He watched as they came and went, like figures in a dream. One by one, they materialized, etched against the beige cloud behind them.

At two hundred and fifty feet, the lead Indian raised a hand. The Indians slowed, walking their horses another hundred feet. One Apache dismounted. He handed his reins to another, then waited for three or four more to join him on the ground.

Chance held his breath. The Apaches on foot approached the wagons. Two of the white men advanced to meet the warriors. A parley, maybe an argument, judging by the vigorous hand gestures, was followed by some sort of agreement. The entire group moved to the rear of one of the wagons.

One of the white men leaned in and tugged something toward him. Its end appeared. A flat wooden box. Chance was confused. It didn't look like any whiskey crate he'd ever seen. It looked familiar though, vaguely. He wracked his memory, but before he figured it out, the crate was broken open. And then he knew—rifles. The bastards were selling guns!

The Apaches examined one of the rifles, a new Winchester from the looks of it. They passed it around. Each man taking a turn at sighting it, working the lever. The magazine was loaded and three or four sharp cracks rolled across the valley floor. Then, so suddenly he couldn't believe he was actually watching it, the mounted Apaches charged. Furious volleys of gunshots, a blur of massed sound, thundered far below him, and Chance watched in amazement.

The white men, clearly taken by surprise, barely got off a shot. And it was over as quickly as it had begun. Indians scrambled into the wagons and released the brakes. Chance watched, still not sure he hadn't imagined it, as everything, wagons, Apaches, horses and all, slowly swam back into the shimmering blur and disappeared. Everything except the six bleeding bodies.

Chance shook his head in disbelief. He looked at the sky, wondering if there could be some explanation there for what he had just witnessed. But there was nothing. Nothing but a lone buzzard, its huge wings no longer flapping as it began the long, slow glide. But there was no hurry. Not now.

13

CHANCE STOOD THERE looking down at the bodies. Once, he took his eyes away to stare after the vanished Apaches, but there was no point. He could see nothing, and he could do nothing. And part of him was glad he had been there to see it. He knew someone would try to make heroes of the men, but they didn't deserve it.

He knew he should bury them. Custom, even propriety, demanded it. But they didn't deserve that, either. What they deserved was exactly what they got. He searched the bodies quickly, looking for proof of identity. He found little. But it was enough. He stuffed the meager papers into his pocket and climbed into the saddle. When he looked up, several more buzzards had begun their descent.

He didn't look back. Not even once.

He had to get the news to Crook, and quickly. But first he had to see to Jenny and the boys. And warn the town. He would pass through Cotton Springs on the way. He would tell Slattery, and it would be the deputy's problem. He could go home and make sure they all survived until the army managed to get itself in motion.

The sun seemed hotter than usual. He felt it on his back, and a peculiar throbbing, like a fist hammered at him, made him tremble in every limb. He felt as if the reins would slip from his hands, or like his head would separate itself from his body and float off toward the sky, like a soap-bubble in the sun.

And when he moved down out of the high desert, he was pushing his horse harder than he should. He slowed it to a walk, finally conscious of the unreasonable pace he'd been setting. Looking up at the sky again, he cursed aloud. It was inhumanly hot, hotter than any man should have to endure. It seemed like a punishment from a particularly vicious judge. He cringed at the thought, knowing what his father's brother would say. But the Reverend Mr. Chance was safe in Ohio. He didn't have to live here, to bear the unbearable, and endure the unendurable. Religion was a comfort in Ohio. Here, it was a cruel joke.

He jerked his canteen free, unscrewed the cap, slowing his horse even more. Tipping the bitter metal mouth of the canteen above his open mouth, he leaned back a bit in the saddle. The warm water tasted of salts, and he felt grit on his tongue. But he was so thirsty. He had to have more. Swirling the remaining water, he gauged the contents, judged he had an inch or two left, and took another pull, leaning his head back even further.

That's when he saw the smoke.

A thick, greasy black rope, it coiled up toward the blue-white sky, slightly bent and beginning to broaden just a little as it climbed. On top of the dense column, just a fringe had begun to spread out and dissipate. It hadn't been burning long. It looked like it wasn't that far, four or five miles.

Mentally, he ran the inventory. What was there between here and the fire? What that would give off that kind of smoke?

He knew then, but didn't want to believe it. With a cry that sounded more animal than human, he drove his spurs deep into his mount's flanks, startling the horse and sending it forward in a single spurt from near motionlessness to a full gallop.

He covered the seven miles in one screaming nightmare. A second column of smoke sprang up beside the first. By the time his house came into view he was hoarse, his throat raw. The smoke was thick now, the house itself a block of orange flames. The barn was burning too, its roof already gone, its walls smothered in thick sheets of red and yellow.

He could hear gunshots now, sporadic firing, a pitched battle. Dead ahead, two men crouched behind an overturned wagon. He leapt from his horse, dragging the Winchester with him. He hit the ground running, lost his balance, and fell to his knees. Scrambling to his feet, he started to rush past the wagon, but someone, he didn't know who, reached out and grabbed his ankles. He fell headlong as a volley of shots peppered the front of the wagon from somewhere to the left of the house.

"Damn it, Dalton, you'll get yourself killed, boy."

He recognized the voice. It was Warren Montrose.

"Jenny," he said. "My boys, they're in the house." He tired to break free, but Montrose threw his weight on top of him and pinned him from behind.

"You can't even get close, Dalton. You can't, now . . ."

"The hell I can't." He curled like an angry bronco and threw Montrose to one side. Scrambling to his feet, he crawled out of the mayor's reach. Another volley of shots ripped at the dirt around the wagon, but Chance ignored it. Charging straight on, he kept low, angling toward a clump of scrub oak. He saw bits of leaf fly in the air as he brought the oak between him and the source of the shots.

Chance dove headfirst, crept up close to the low-hanging limbs and burrowed through the foliage enough to get a closer look. As near as he could tell, the firing was coming from some cottonwoods dead center between the house and barn, but some fifty or sixty feet behind either building.

He turned to look back at Montrose, who was peeking out from behind the wagon, his head partly obscured by its weathered tongue.

"How many, Warren?" he shouted.

"Four or five, near as we can make out. Might be one more with the horses back there, but I ain't sure."

"You seen 'em?"

"Hell, yes, I seen 'em."

"Who are they?"

"Who the hell you think they are, Dalton? Apaches, for Christ's sake. Just like I told you."

Chance surveyed the open ground ahead of him. If the Apaches were confined to the cottonwoods, they had only a narrow alley to shoot through. If he could get off to the right, he'd be wide open for ten or fifteen yards, but then he'd have the house between him and them. He might be able to get close enough to break in the door.

He had to try.

"I'm gonna get closer, Warren."

"Dalton, don't . . ."

But Chance wasn't listening. He rolled to the right, holding the Winchester in both hands extended far ahead of him to cut down on the drag. He sensed bullets striking all around him for a few seconds, and closed his eyes as he rolled to keep the dust out of them and to keep from getting dizzy.

He spread his legs to brake his roll, then in almost the same motion, scrambled to his feet and started toward the house. Behind him, he could hear Montrose and the other man lay down a covering fire. He hoped to God Montrose was a better shot than he was a mayor, or he'd take one in the back.

As he drew close, he could feel the terrible heat on the exposed skin of his face and hands. The wood popped and crackled, small showers of sparks arced out and away with every exploded pocket of sap and gas. The door itself was on fire, but not burning as furiously.

Putting his head down, Chance charged onto the porch. He slammed into the door and bounced off, nearly falling. His sore shoulder spurted molten lead through his upper body. Only dimly aware of the bullet holes in the door, he charged into it again. He felt the searing heat of the charred wood on his skin, but this time the door gave way, sending him sprawling into the front room.

The house was full of smoke, and the thick air

made him gag as he tried to breathe. Staying on the floor, he crept toward the back rooms. He could hear more gunshots both ahead and behind him, as Montrose continued to trade fire with the Apaches.

"Jenny." He shouted her name once, twice, three times. No answer. "Dalton?" He waited for his elder son to respond. Again, he heard nothing. "Curt . . ." He called the little one's name. But this time, he knew no one would answer. Shielding his face with his arm as best he could, he crawled toward the bedrooms. The first one was empty, except for the choking cloud of thick smoke.

The other was also full of smoke. He crawled inside just as the back window broke, the glass tinkling onto the ground inside and out. The window frame burst into flame. He swept at the smoke with one desperate arm, succeeding only in swirling the cloud a little at its bottom edge. The heat was almost overwhelming.

"Jenny?"

Again no answer. He squirmed around the bed, bruising his elbow on the bed leg. And he found them.

He crept closer, almost afraid of the still forms lying in a tight knot in the corner. The shotgun lay on the floor next to Jenny's outstretched leg. Her arms held the boys close.

There was blood all over the back of Dalton Junior's shirt. Only dimly aware that the firing had stopped, he gathered the boys in his arms and stood up, ignoring the thick smoke, and ran toward the front of the house. He nearly knocked Montrose over as he plunged out into the clear air.

Chance thrust the boys into the mayor's arms and turned back to the house. The man with Montrose grabbed him, but Chance turned on him and swung from the heels. He caught the man, realizing in the same instant it was Dan Hastings, flush on the jaw. Hastings staggered and fell, and Chance rushed back into the house as Montrose called to him to stop.

Back in the bedroom, again on his stomach, he crawled to her body. The blood made him gag. He rolled on his side and vomited. The thick fluid started to bubble where it lay against the wall. It would be only a matter of minutes before the floor, too, burst into flame. Chance lay there sobbing, one hand on Jenny's waist. He didn't want to move. What was the point, he thought? Better to stay there with her, let it all end now. There was no way he could live without her, without his sons.

Chance got to his knees and crawled into the corner. He hugged her lifeless body to him and sat there, his back flat against the wall.

He was still sitting there when Montrose and Hastings burst into the room. They tried to drag him away, but he wouldn't let go of Jenny. "No," he bellowed, getting to his feet. "No."

"Dalton," Montrose begged, "you have to get out of here. Dan will bring Jenny out."

"No." Again. And again.

He dropped to one knee and lifted her. He realized the back of her dress was hot. Her hair was matted with blood. He staggered toward the door, and turned to get through the narrow opening. Out through the front, again screaming, "No."

And out into the setting sun. He saw the boys, lying on the small patch of grass Jenny had tried so hard to grow. There was just enough room for her body, and he staggered toward it, knelt down, then collapsed, sitting there with Jenny in his lap. He brushed the blood-stiffened hair away from her brow, kissed her forehead. The smell of the blood assaulted him, came away on his lips.

Montrose and Hastings stood over him, their hands limp at their sides. "Dalton, you alright? Dalton?" Montrose asked.

Chance looked up as if he couldn't believe the question. Then he closed his eyes and shook his head. "No," he said. It was a simple whisper.

"Dan," Montrose said, "you better ride into town and get Zack Morely out here."

"No," Chance said. "No undertaker. I'll bury them myself, right here."

"Dalton, you can't . . ."

"I can do what I want, Warren. Leave me alone."

"Them savages'll pay for this, you mark my words."

"Somebody will pay," Chance said. "But not now. Go on, leave me be."

"Them Apaches might still be out there."

"Maybe, Warren. Maybe. That'll be fine."

"You want me and Dan to help you?"

"It's my family, Warren. Mine! I'll do it."

Chance looked past the two men at the blazing barn, then at the house. As he watched, the roof fell in, sending a column of sparks high into the air. They climbed into the darkening sky like small orange stars, and winked out one by one.

He lay Jenny down beside the boys. Getting to his feet, he walked toward the barn. The rails of the small corral were already beginning to burn up close where they joined the wall of the barn. He found a shovel leaning against the fence and walked on between the blazing house and barn, all that was left of his life, going up in smoke.

14

CHANCE FINISHED SMOOTHING the dirt, threw the shovel aside and sat down to wait for the sun. He listened to the sound of night dying away, watched the big owl that nested in the small grove of cottonwoods glide to its nest, then the first birds beginning to stir. The stars went out and the sky turned gray. When the sun peeked over the mountains to the east, it stained his hands bright red. He looked at them dumbly, tried to wipe the color away, then let them fall in his lap where they lay like dead things.

He was chilled through. A thin glaze of dew glistened on the fine hairs on his arms and the backs of his hands. He felt stiff, and his breathing was painful. He walked to the well and cranked the handle after using a thick green glass jar to prime the pump, and filled a bucket. He watched the

morning brighten for a few moments, then knelt
down and plunged his face and hands into the pail,
splattering cold water all over himself, rubbing his
face briskly. He stuck his head into the bucket for
a second, then lifted his head. He let the water run
down his collar and stream down over his face and
chest.

It smelled of ashes. The smokey scent clung to
his hair and clothes. The ruins still smoldered behind him. Now and then a board would shift, or
something would pop. He tried his best to ignore
it. Plunging his head back into the pail, he shook
it, trying to wash away the stale stench of the fire.
This time, when he straightened up, someone
stood beside him.

When the knee-high moccasins registered, he
reached for his gun even before turning to look.
Lone Wolf stared down at him.

"I am sorry," he said.

"Get the hell out of here, you bastard."

The Apache's face betrayed no emotion. The Indian waited. Chance stood up, waving the gun.
"What the hell do you want? Haven't you done
enough already?"

Lone Wolf sighed. "I am sorry for this," he said,
pointing to the heaps of ashes. "And for this." He
indicated the freshly turned earth.

"I don't need sympathy from an Apache,"
Chance said.

Lone Wolf ignored the implications. "I was afraid this would happen," he said. "Juh is a cruel man."

"Juh? Is that his name? Where is he?"

The Indian swept a hand to the south, embracing half the planet. "Out there somewhere," he said.

"Then go find him."

"Juh is not the problem."

"Then who is?"

"Tucker Wiley."

"Tucker Wiley didn't slaughter my family. Apaches did."

"You don't understand. Wiley steals from the Apaches. And then he pretends to be their friend, selling them things they need. He is getting fat on the army and fatter still on the Apache."

"I don't care about that. What I care about is finding the men who did this . . ." he looked around at the ruins of his life, his eyes skirting the graves but never quite focusing on them. "That's what I care about."

"You are wrong."

He felt his finger quivering on the trigger. "What do you know about it? It's not your family in the ground."

"No," he said.

"Then what do you want?"

Lone Wolf looked at him and Chance glared

back. He sensed that the Apache wanted to tell him something, but couldn't, for reasons Chance couldn't guess.

"If you have nothing more to say, I suggest you get back to Fort Apache. You won't be safe around here after this morning."

"I have done nothing."

"That won't matter to the people around here. Hell, I'm not sure it even matters to me."

"I thought you were different."

Chance laughed bitterly. "Nobody's different. Nobody. We are what we are. We're like our people. Do you understand?"

Lone Wolf looked blank.

Chance tried to find the words. "What I mean is . . . I'm a white man. As far as Juh is concerned, that's all that matters. If I *was* different, and I'm not at all sure of that, it didn't matter to him. It didn't help my family."

Lone Wolf nodded. "You are saying that if Apaches do not notice the difference in white men, then white men won't notice them in Apaches."

"Precisely."

"And you are a white man and you do not care about the difference?"

Chance nodded.

Lone Wolf took a deep breath. He extended a hand, but Chance just looked at it. After a long moment, the Indian let it drop. He turned without a word. "Hightail it to the fort, if you know what's good for you," Chance shouted.

When the Indian was gone, he walked to his horse and climbed into the saddle. All he had to his name was on the back of his horse. Chance didn't give a damn what happened to him from now on. All he wanted was revenge. On the ride into town, the fury in him slowly congealed, like ice forming on the surface of a stream. By the time he rode into Cotton Springs, the rage was a solid block of ice deep in his gut.

He felt nothing.

The town was alive with gossips, people standing in knots all along the main street. As he rode past, they stared at him, some starting toward him a step or two then, arrested by something in his face, they froze and backed away. No one said a word, not even the obligatory expression of condolence. Chance noticed, but he didn't mind.

Words meant nothing now. Deeds were all that mattered. And there was nothing anyone could do for Jenny or Dalton Junior or Curt. Nothing anyone could do for him. He dismounted in front of Red Malone's saloon, tied up and stepped onto the walk. He paused for just a second at the door, pushed inside and walked to the bar. The noise stopped completely. The conversations, so animated a second before, had suddenly died.

Malone watched him from behind the bar.

Chance took a stool and dropped a silver dollar on the polished wood. "Whiskey," he said.

"Dalton, maybe you . . ."

"Whiskey, Red. Now."

Malone nodded. He turned to pull a bottle from the shelf under the mirror, poured two fingers of Jim Beam and replaced the bottle without looking. He reached out to nudge the coin back toward Chance. "You don't need this," he said. "Put it in your pocket."

Chance ignored the coin. He downed the whiskey in a single swallow. Rapping the glass on the bar, he said, "One more, Red."

Malone poured, then stepped back to lean against the shelf. He watched Chance nervously. Slowly, the conversations resumed. The voices sounded brittle, the humor forced, the volume a little too loud. Everyone in the bar was trying to pretend, except for Malone.

And Dalton Chance.

He had a third drink, then listened to the conversation. Everyone but Malone seemed to have forgotten he was there. He knew it was because no one really knew what to say. And the stiffness of his shoulders, the look of his face, were enough to intimidate anyone who thought he might be able to offer some comfort.

He wasn't drunk, but the pain was numbed a bit. He wanted to crawl right inside the bottle and

drink his way out. But that would just postpone
what he knew he had to do. While he nursed a
fourth whiskey, a handful of men came bustling
into the saloon. They took a table, scraping back
the chairs and joking among themselves. At first,
he was just annoyed by their apparent insensitivity.
Then he realized that they had no reason to know
what he had done that morning, or to care why.
But it didn't matter. He found himself listening,
looking for an excuse to pick a fight.

When they had their first round of drinks in
front of them, they settled down. They were still
talking, but not so loudly. He heard a few scraps
that piqued his interest. San Carlos was mentioned, as was the name Juh. And Wiley. Just those
two syllables. It could have been a first name or a
last, but somehow he knew they referred to Tucker
Wiley.

"Connie wasn't nothing but rags and bones,"
one of them was saying. "Them buzzards was all
over the place when we got there."

Chance cocked his head without turning to look
at them. He didn't want them to know he was pay-
ing any attention.

"Served the bastard right," another one said.
"Told him he was crazy to trust that damn Injun."

"Hell, I don't trust none of 'em, myself," the
first man said.

"Keep your voices down, you idiots." This was

a third voice, a new one. It was deep and assured. He guessed it must have belonged to the biggest of the four, the one who had led the way into the saloon.

Chance was all ears, now. Connie must have been one of the teamsters he'd watched the day before. "Glad it wasn't me," one of the men said. "Wiley wanted me to go, but I told him I wasn't interested."

"You better go to church come Sunday, Mason. Thank your lucky stars."

"Lucky stars, hell. That was common sense. I told Wiley he's playin' with fire. Sonofabitch don't give a damn. Wants the money."

"Keep your voices *down*, dammit." Again, that deep voice. This time Chance turned around. One of the men looked at him, whispered something to the others, and their conversation stopped altogether.

The one watching him was a big man, probably over two hundred pounds. He scowled at Chance, but Chance kept on watching.

"You want something?" the man asked. His was the deep voice.

Chance didn't say anything.

Malone grabbed Chance's sleeve. "Don't pay them any attention, Dalton."

"I asked if you wanted something," the baritone said again, this time pushing his chair back.

Chance continued to stare. He felt Malone's hand on his arm, but he paid no attention to it.

"Because we're trying to have a conversation, here. Don't need nobody peekin' over our shoulders," the man continued. He stood up, and the other three turned in their chairs.

Chance heard movement behind him. Malone going for his hog-leg, he thought. But he still didn't turn around.

The big man was moving closer now. "He don't mean nothing, Mister," Malone said. "Why don't you just sit on back down?"

"Don't want to sit down till I straighten out something," he answered.

"Look . . ."

"No, *you* look. I asked the man to mind his own business. He don't know how to do that, then I got to teach him."

"Who's Connie?" Chance asked.

"None of your damn business." The big man moved another step. Chance could see that his fingers were twitching as his gunhand moved closer to the butt of his Colt.

"He's dead, isn't he?" Chance asked.

"I told you to mind your own business."

"Why don't you tell everybody where he died. And how?"

"Shut up."

The big man squared up now.

"Where's Tucker Wiley?" Chance asked.

"Go to hell!"

"He selling guns to Apaches this morning?"

The big man moved, but Chance was quicker. He charged off his stool and knocked the big man backward. Chance carried him to the floor and scrambled up until he was astride the larger man, who outweighed him by twenty pounds or so. Chance locked his hands over the man's throat and leaned into his grip with stiff arms.

"Where is he, you bastard?"

The big man struggled to break the grip, his fingers clawing at the back of Chance's hands. The three men at the table started to get up, but Malone brought a sawed-off shotgun out from under the bar.

"Chance, let him go," the bartender said. "Dalton? Let him up now . . ."

"Where's Wiley? Where is he?" Chance rocked forward putting all his weight behind the stranglehold. "Where is he, you bastard?"

Malone moved around the bar. "Dalton, come on, now, you're gonna kill him."

"I *will* kill him, he doesn't tell me what I want to know."

"Let him up, Dalton. Come on, now."

"Ask those boys at the table who Connie is. Go on, ask them."

Malone started to argue, but Chance turned to

look at him, and one look at his face convinced
Malone he was serious.

"Who's Connie?" Malone asked.

They didn't answer. "I'll strangle the sonofabitch," Chance shouted. "You hear me? I'll
strangle the sonofabitch. Tell him. Tell him about
the guns. Tell him about Wiley selling guns to the
Apaches."

They shook their heads, and Chance squeezed
harder. The man under him was unconscious now,
his face turning red, his lips turning blue and trembling. He was drooling.

"Tell him!" Chance shouted.

One of the men went for his gun, but Chance
was ready. He drew his own Colt and fired once,
catching the man high on the shoulder. "Tell him
or I'll kill all of you," he screamed. "Tell him!"

One of the others nodded. "Alright, alright."

Chance walked toward him, his pistol cocked,
and waved it under his nose. "You tell him all of
it," he said.

The patrons in the saloon were closing into a
tight circle. Chance was only dimly aware of them.
He watched the man, his lips quivering, his voice
refusing to come. Chance jabbed the muzzle of the
Colt into the man's upper lip and pushed.

"I, unh . . . yeah. Wiley's unh . . ."

But Chance didn't wait to hear it all. He slipped
through the crowd and out the door.

15

CHANCE RODE HARD all the way to Fort Apache. When he broke into the compound, he slowed his horse halfway across, skidding to a halt right in front of the headquarters building. The same corporal he'd seen two days before was on the door. The young soldier took one look at him and decided to stand back. Chance barged into the office, making straight for Crook's inner office.

The door was closed, but Chance didn't bother to knock. He swung the door back and it banged against the wall hard enough to rattle the glass. Crook was behind his desk, talking to two officers, a major and a captain, sitting in ladderback chairs pulled up close to it. A map was spread out on the desk, and Crook suspended a pointing finger long enough to look at Chance in amazement.

The general scowled. "Sergeant," he said. "I

didn't expect to see you again so soon. But you'll have to excuse me. We were in the middle of discussing something rather urgent." Then, as Chance's appearance registered, he asked, "Anything wrong?"

"Damn right there is." He glared at the two officers. "I'd like to speak to the general alone, if you don't mind."

The captain seemed confused. The major, though, was bristling. "Look here, man, you can't . . ."

"No, you look. I want to talk to General Crook. Get out of here."

The major stood up, but Crook took command. "Major, perhaps we can adjourn for a few minutes, humh?"

"But General, we can't allow . . ."

"In a few minutes, Major. Please."

The captain was already standing at the door. The major, though, took his time, stopping once to glare at Chance. Chance turned away, afraid he would attack the man if he said a single word. The major then stalked out, and the captain closed the door gently behind him.

Chance was pacing like a madman. Crook seemed genuinely concerned. He stood up to walk around the front of his desk. "Now, Dalton, why don't you tell me what's on your mind?"

"Where is Tucker Wiley?"

"I'm sure I don't know. You mean to tell me you barge in here like a lunatic to ask me where he is?"

"Not exactly."

"Then what?" Crook was plainly annoyed. His voice took on an edge, his tone became brassy, his words were clipped. "Explain yourself."

Chance collapsed into one of the chairs. Crook stood looking down at him, swept away on the torrent of words. When it stopped, Crook sat down. "And you're sure about this?" he asked.

"I saw it with my own eyes. The guns, then the shooting. Three wagon loads. I don't know what was in them, except for the case of rifles, but . . ."

"And they were Tucker Wiley's men?"

Chance fished the papers out of his pocket. He handed them to Crook. The general examined them carefully. Satisfied, he set them down on the corner of his desk. "I recognize two or three of the names. But it still doesn't prove Wiley knew anything about it. How do you know the weapons weren't stolen?"

"Damn it, General, how much proof do you need before you can do something."

Crook laid a hand on Chance's shoulder. "Mr. Chance, you've been through a lot. I understand your impatience but it may be just that. You want vengeance. But that won't change anything. And in your haste, you may be barking up the wrong tree, simply because it's the closest."

Chance was exasperated. He tried not to show it, but failed miserably. "Look, General. One of your own men knows the whole story. Ask him, why don't you. See if he agrees with what I've just told you."

"One of my men? Who? Who is it?"

"One of your scouts, an Apache. Ki-Lo-Tah, his name is."

"Just a minute. You stay right there." Crook moved to the door, jerked it open, and Chance saw the major, still frowning, pacing anxiously outside. The major started to say something, but Crook shook him off. "Not now, Major. Lieutenant?"

"Yes, sir?"

Chance could hear but not see the respondent. Crook said, "I want to talk to one of the Apaches, Ki-Lo-Tah. Now."

"Yes, sir."

The lieutenant was a blur of blue and gold as he rushed past the open door. A moment later, the front door banged and Crook was back. "I'll have to ask for your patience, Mr. Chance. I've sent for the man in question. But it might take a while to locate him."

"I heard. And I'll wait."

"Good. Now, let me ask you a few questions, if I might."

Chance shrugged. "Suit yourself, General."

"I usually do, as you may remember." Chance didn't respond and Crook pushed on. "Now, if I understand you correctly, you claim Tucker Wiley is selling both whiskey and guns to renegade Apaches. Is that correct?"

"Yes, sir."

"But the one thing you haven't told me is why. Why would he be doing such a horrible thing?"

"I can't answer that, general. I have no idea. I know what Ki-Lo-Tah thinks. But he can speak for himself."

"Why don't you save us some time? Tell me what he thinks."

"Alright," Chance shrugged. "He thinks Wiley is trying to stir up trouble. Wiley does a lot of business with the Army. If the Army were to leave the Fort, it would cost him a lot of money. So, he makes sure you don't leave by making sure you have somebody to fight, somebody to chase, some reason to stay here."

"Does that make sense to you, Dalton?"

"Hell, general, I'm not a businessman. But I know one thing. Greed will make a man do some crazy things. You know that better than I do. Hell, your whole career has been cleaning up after greedy bastards. They make a mess, somebody gets killed, and you have to restore order. Isn't that how it works? Wasn't that the story with the Sioux? Wasn't that the story with the Cheyenne? And the Kiowa? And the Comanche? Why should it be any different here?"

"You're suggesting Wiley puts his personal enrichment ahead of the lives and property of the residents of this Territory, both white and red?"

"I'm not suggesting anything. You asked me to tell you what Ki-Lo-Tah thinks. I just did."

"Has it occurred to you that Ki-Lo-Tah may simply be attempting to excuse his tribe? After all, they are his family, many of them."

"He's your man, General. You'd know that better than I would."

Crook was silent for a long time. He kept glancing at the door. Chance studied the general as he paced back and forth, his hands folded behind his back. It seemed to Chance the man had aged five years in fifteen minutes. The cheeks sagged a little more, the eyes sparkled less. Even the general's voice was less firm than it had been.

Crook wheeled suddenly and confronted Chance. "Mr. Chance, what do you want me to do? I mean if your charges can be substantiated."

"Stay out of my way."

"I can't do that. You know I can't, Dalton."

"Hanging's too quick. I figure Ki-Lo-Tah can teach me a few tricks, make the bastard hang around a while, and suffer a little bit. That would help some."

"You don't mean that."

"Begging the General's pardon, but I most certainly do. I buried my wife and two sons this morning, General. Nothing that happens to me now matters at all, and whatever it is, it won't hurt as much."

There was a knock on the office door. "Come

in, dammit," Crook bellowed, louder than he intended. The lieutenant opened the door cautiously, peering around its edge. Crook waved him in impatiently. "Well, did you find him?"

The lieutenant shook his head. "No sir."

"Why not?"

The young officer swallowed hard. "He's gone, sir."

"Gone, what the hell do you mean, gone?"

"I mean he left this morning, sir. Tore up his enlistment form, handed it to Captain Parmenter, packed his fear and left."

"Where in the hell did he go? And why in blazes didn't I hear about this until now?"

"I don't know, sir. I'm only relaying the information from the captain, sir."

"Get Parmenter over here on the double."

"Yes sir." The lieutenant was too flustered to salute. He backed out the door, leaving it open. Chance watched the major, still pacing back and forth outside. He started toward the door, but Chance got up and pushed it closed. He heard the major curse.

"Chance, I swear, if you're mixed up with this Ki-Lo-Tah in some crazy scheme, I'll have you in jail so long you'll never see the light of day as a free man."

Chance exploded. "Damn it, General, I came here two days ago to warn you about this. You wanted to take your time. Now I come back, and you want to read *me* the riot act. It seems to me like you're the one's barking up the closest tree, General. Now, you want to arrest me, you better forget about it. I don't mind telling you, anybody tries to stop me, I'll kill him."

"Chance, sit down, dammit."

"Sorry, sir. I'm not in the army anymore."

"You're in my office, and you'll do what I say."

"No, sir. I'm leaving now. You find out what you can from your captain and you do what you have to. I'll do the same. But if I get to Tucker Wiley before you do, he's a dead man."

"Chance, you can't . . ."

"Good afternoon, General."

Chance jerked the door open. He headed for the front. Crook ran after him, shouting, "Chance, dammit, you come back here. Major, stop him."

Chance heard footsteps and turned as the major reached out for him. He pulled his Colt and cocked it. The major stopped in his tracks. "I'll kill you Major, you take one more step. Understand?"

The major nodded. Over his shoulder to Crook, he said, "Shall I call the guard, General?"

"No, Major. Come into my office."

"But . . ."

"Now, Major." Crook looked at Chance. "I hope you know what you're doing, Dalton."

"So do I, General. So do I."

16

CHANCE CAMPED FOR THE NIGHT bone weary and half mad. Frustrated by Crook's insistence on procedures, and angry enough to cut his own throat if no one came to hand, he lay down next to his small fire and watched the flames. Everything he had on earth was gone. And nobody seemed to give a damn about it. Everyone had his own agenda.

Fine, he thought. I always took care of myself, solved my own problems. I can still do it.

The fire crackled and the flames danced. Staring into them through hooded eyes, he felt himself drifting away, not to sleep, but to someplace else, someplace he'd never been. For a moment, he thought he was watching the house burn, and he thought of Jenny. And he thought of Dalton Junior. And little Curt, who needed a haircut.

Wiley was supposed to be down south, somewhere near the Alamosa River. It was Apache country, and it was likely that Juh and his bands would be headed that way. It would be too much to hope that he could catch them both together. But maybe, if there was a God, and if He was . . .

But there was no God. There couldn't be. If there were, he wouldn't be lying here now. He'd be home. With Jenny.

He had no plan, and he had no help. But somehow, he knew, he was going to get to Wiley, and to Juh, even if it killed him. He wished now that he had been more willing to listen to Lone Wolf, but that was water under the bridge. He was as alone as a man could be, but that was a small blessing. Nothing could get to him now. There was no one to worry about, nothing for him to think about except revenge.

He suspected Crook was going to send a detachment after him. That was alright. One man, alone, could hide forever in the mountains and canyons. He wasn't an Apache, but he was smart and he was strong. And, more than anything else that mattered, he was determined. And what was a handful of soldiers, after all? An annoyance, nothing more. They couldn't control the Apaches, and they couldn't control him. If he had to, he would fight them, too. That was the essence of it. Nothing mattered anymore.

He closed his eyes, still in shock, still grieving, but knowing that when he woke in the morning, and every morning for the rest of his life, there was only one thing he had to do. And when he had done it, they could bury him. Alive or dead, it wouldn't matter.

Once or twice during the night, a sound, or some imagined sound, ruptured his fitful sleep. He would lay there listening, trying to decide what was real. His head was full of imaginary sounds, and remembered sounds. Gunshots, crackling timber, falling rocks, screams. All of them crowded in on him, one drowning out the other, until the constant din faded away under its own weight. Then he would drift off again, feeling the earth shift beneath him, or fall away.

He seemed to be floating above himself, looking down at his inert body beside the dying fire. He thought how pitiful he was, brushed the thought away, and came back to it. He seemed inadequate, a failure of the worst kind—a man who couldn't even protect what was his, or those who needed his protection.

Each time he awoke and opened his eyes, the same deep blue-black sky pressed down on him, scarred by the same stars. The constellations moved, and he could gauge the passing time, but it moved too slowly to suit him. He wanted to be awake and up, moving to keep from falling through the earth and disappearing as he so richly deserved to do.

Once an owl woke him, its cry almost human. He lay there watching the sky, waiting for the shadow to glide by above him, for the beat of wings thick as leather, but it never came, and he remembered his father telling him how owls had special feathers that made no noise. He felt foolish having forgotten, and it hurt to remember the man who had taken care of him as he had been unable to take care of his own sons.

And when he awoke for the fourth or fifth time, he'd lost count, the blue-black was gone, replaced by an endless gray. It was only an hour before dawn. He turned in his bedroll, looked at the fire and started to drift off again. But something didn't seem right. The fire should have been out. He was wide awake in a second, motionless, listening.

He thought he could hear breathing somewhere in the pre-dawn shadows, but refused to turn his head. Listening and listening, until he thought his head would burst with the strain, he heard nothing but the crackling flames.

So slowly he wasn't even sure he was moving at all, he slid a hand down along his hip, groping for the Colt in his bedroll. He found it after an eternity, closed his fingers around the grip, and slid it back along his body. Not until it was scant inches from the edge of the blanket did he sit up, and then, without seeing anything, roll to the side, struggling to get free of the bedroll.

He saw the man only then.

"You don't sleep well," Lone Wolf said.

"What do you want?" Chance was angry and he was embarrassed. Fantasizing about revenge half the night, and an Apache rebuilt a fire not ten feet away and he didn't know it. Some avenger, he thought. He said, "Leave me alone."

"I need you," the Apache said.

"I don't need you."

Chance saw Lone Wolf smile for the first time since meeting him. The Indian threw a stick on the fire. It clicked against the others and sent a shower of sparks up into the brightening gray. He didn't say anything. He didn't have to.

"Alright, so you could have killed me, so what."

"Juh *would* kill you."

"But he's not here."

"Are you sure?"

"Are you?"

"No."

"But you think he is?"

"No."

"Do you know where he is?"

"He has gone to Taza, in the Alamosa."

"Taza won't help him."

"Yes he will. Cochise taught his people not to make war on the white man. But that was before.

Now, the white man wants to move the Chiricahua, take away the reservation and make them come to San Carlos. Everything is different, now. And Cochise is dead. Juh and Loco and Victorio and Geronimo are not Cochise."

Chance was getting interested in spite of himself. He was still angry, and still didn't trust the scout. But what he said made sense. All bets were off, now. If one side could break an agreement, the other side would no longer feel obliged to honor it.

"Why do you need me?" he asked. "I can't get to Taza. There is no reason he would listen to me. Or is there?"

"You can go to the white man's villages. I cannot. You can ask questions. With what you learn and what I know, we can find Juh and we can find Tucker Wiley."

"And I suppose you think you can handle Juh, is that it?"

"No."

"Then what?"

"I can tell him to surrender."

"Over my dead body. He killed my family. You think I can forget that? Maybe you can, but I can't. And I won't."

"It was his rancheria the white men burned. He was wrong to kill people who did not do it. But he knows the whites do not know the difference between one Apache and another, or between an Apache warrior and an Apache child."

"And I'm supposed to give a damn about that?"

"To understand . . ."

Chance got to his feet and walked to the edge of the creek. He knelt on the sandy bank and leaned over to rinse his face and hands, took a drink, and straightened up. He thought about what Lone Wolf said. Part of him agreed that they could be useful to one another. And part of him rebelled at the very thought of cooperating with a representative of the tribe that had taken his family.

He sat down on the sand, his back to Lone Wolf, and stroked his chin. Three days growth of whiskers made him feel uncivilized, as if he was stripping away whatever had made him different from the Indian. If the rules were changing, and he was changing, then maybe . . . but he couldn't decide. He wanted revenge and he didn't care what he had to do to get it. But would it be revenge at all if an Apache helped him attain it, or would it be one final capitulation, one final proof that he had been defeated?

He turned to look at the Apache, still squatting on the far side of the fire. Lone Wolf was staring into the flames, as if mesmerized. He glanced once at Chance, as if to gauge his response to the proposal, but his face was as stony as ever. The black eyes, all but invisible in the grayness, caught the firelight. They glittered like fireflies, occasionally winking out when he blinked.

Chance straightened up and looked at the sky. He sighed once, and sucked his teeth. He felt all but paralyzed, as if either answer would be the wrong one. If he said yes, he could get to Juh and Wiley, but surrender to inadequacy. But if he said no, he might waste what little life he had left in him and fail to achieve anything at all. It was a devil's bargain.

And he made his choice.

Walking back to the fire, he stepped past it and stood over the Apache.

"Suppose I agree?" he asked.

Lone Wolf didn't answer immediately. When he finally spoke, his voice was subdued. "Then we have a chance."

"If I say no, do *you* have a chance? To get Wiley?"

"Yes."

"But it would be better if we work together?"

"Yes."

"Alright," he said, regretting it already, but not knowing what else to do.

17

CHANCE KNEW RIGHT AWAY he couldn't have managed without the Apache. While sitting on his horse, Lone Wolf spotted tracks that Chance had missed on his hands and knees. As a result, they saved time. It also meant they were less likely to ride into an ambush.

They pushed their horses hard, knowing that Juh and his band were probably heading for Mexico. But on the way, they would kill anyone they came across, white and Indian alike. And once they made the border, Chance could forget about finding them. The Apaches had been using the Sierra Madres for years, and were as familiar with Chihuahua and Sonora as they were with New Mexico and Arizona. The advantage belonged to Juh. And according to Lone Wolf, he had some of the most seasoned Apache warriors with him. Unlike many break-outs in the past, this time they travelled unencumbered by women and children. They were free to strike wherever they wanted, without fear that their families would be vulnerable to either the army, or to a posse of vengeful Arizonans.

As nightfall neared on the first day, Chance had learned much from the scout. But he was inexperienced. He could see some things when they were pointed out, but he wouldn't have noticed them if left to his own devices.

Still, he was getting used to the idea of working with the Apache. Lone Wolf spoke only when he had something to say. There was some great reserve in him, a distance, as if his body sat on the horse ahead of Chance but his mind was somewhere else. Chance didn't know whether he was simply thinking ahead, or if he was as mistrustful of Chance as Chance was of him. Probably the latter, he thought. And he nodded to himself. It made sense. They were more alike than he had thought.

Lone Wolf was looking for a campsite now, and they followed a creek, staying in the water. The fewer tracks of their own they left, the less likely the army would catch up with them. It also reduced the possibility of one of Juh's scouts stumbling on them by accident. Lone Wolf explained that a good Apache warrior always knows what is going on behind him, as well as ahead of him. He

said Juh was one of the best, now only second to
Geronimo as the leader of a war party, and maybe
to Nana, who was older and therefore knew more.

With a half-hour of daylight left, he found the
sort of place he was looking for. Without speaking,
he dismounted and took the small, lightweight saddle from his mount. He hobbled both it and his
follow-horse within drinking distance of the creek,
and set about gathering straw and dried leaves for
a makeshift mattress.

Chance climbed down from his own mount,
bone weary and nearly dead on his feet. He gathered some small branches and started to arrange
them for a fire. He noticed Lone Wolf watching
him. When he pulled a match from a waterproof
box in his pocket, the Apache said, "No fire."

"Why not?"

"No fire," he said again. There was no explanation, and Chance was too tired to argue. He turned
his horses out, dropped his saddle near a clump of
scrub oak and sat down with three strips of dried
venison. The meat was stringy and tasted too
much of salt for him, but it was all he had. He
washed it down with some creekwater, then
wrapped himself in his blanket, using the saddle
for a pillow. He was out in a few seconds.

The Apache watched him sleep awhile, sitting
on his haunches and listening. Chance might not
realize it, but the hostiles weren't that far away.

Lone Wolf wanted to see for himself. When he was sure Chance was asleep, he slipped away, walking in the creek for several hundred feet. If they found him, he didn't want to leave a trail that would lead them back to Chance.

He was back in an hour. He debated waking the sleeping man, but decided against it. Chance didn't have his stamina, and he had not slept well, if at all, for days. It was a simple arrangement he had made, but to make it work, he needed Chance strong and alert. Both their lives would depend on it. He could carry him for awhile, but not forever.

He slept lightly, waking every fifteen or twenty minutes. Chance, too, slept only fitfully. The two men, so different, united only for the moment, and only for as long as it took to achieve their individual goals, would go their separate ways. But for the time being, they depended on each other, and neither was happy about it.

Once, Lone Wolf thought about telling Chance that he had lost his sister and two nieces in the attack on Juh's rancheria, but that would be too much like begging. And the Apache never mentioned the dead. Things were changing, but that would be one of the last of the old ways to die. It was too close to the bone to give way so easily. No, Chance would have to learn to trust him, to see that it was a good thing to work together.

When Chance felt the hand on his shoulder, he

was reaching for his gun even before his eyes opened. He saw Lone Wolf hovering above him, and felt the hand close over his mouth. The Indian held a finger to his lips, and Chance nodded that he understood.

The hand was taken away, and Lone Wolf pointed downstream. He held up three fingers. Chance knew some sign language, but he didn't need it to understand this. Three men were close by. Almost certainly Apaches, he thought, because the army was incapable of moving fast enough to have men this close. And the army moved at night only when necessary.

Lone Wolf disappeared into the trees, and Chance crept to the edge of the cottonwood grove. He strained to hear, but there was nothing but a breeze blowing down off the hilltops rustling the leaves. Chance was going crazy sitting still. He felt like he should do something. If he moved into the trees, he ran the risk of letting the Apaches know he was aware of them. That could put Lone Wolf in jeopardy. But sitting on his hands was more than he could bear.

He slipped off his boots and cocked his pistol, then moved into the creek. The water was cold, and the rocky bottom hurt his feet. Moss on some of the larger rocks made the footing treacherous. Once, he slipped, his knee falling into the water with a loud splash.

Chance held his breath, listening for some sign that he'd been heard. When he was sure he hadn't been, he started moving again. There was a partial moon, and he felt naked out in the open, but the creekbank was overgrown almost to the waterline and if he could just keep his footing, he could make more silent progress keeping to the stream.

A horse nickered off to his left. He stopped and leaned toward the sound, straining his eyes into the leaves, but he couldn't see anything. The horse moved restlessly, its hooves thumping hollowly on the ground.

He had gone about a hundred yards, when he heard another sound, this one a low gurgle, like water running down a short rapids. It lasted for a few seconds, then died away. He checked the stream ahead, but the surface of the water was unbroken. Neither bank showed a feeder or tributary of any kind. He stayed motionless, only his eyes moving. He was aware of his own breathing. He could see his chest rising and falling, and his gun hand trembling the least little bit. His feet were getting numb now, and he worried that he wouldn't be able to move quickly if he had to.

Working his way toward the bank, he found a large rock just above the waterline. Its surface was gritty with dried lichens. They gave him secure footing, and it felt good to get his feet out of the numbing cold. A low-hanging willow branch ob-

structed his view downstream, and he reached out
to pull it toward him, holding his breath to listen
for the first sign of the branch snapping. The leaves
rustled stiffly, and he cursed silently, chewing his
lip in annoyance.

He managed to get the branch behind him, brac-
ing it with the back of his left arm. Something
caught his eye downstream, and he froze. He felt
exposed, and wanted to crouch, but couldn't, for
fear of letting the branch snap back. It would cut
off his field of vision, and even the noise might be
enough to alert a wary Apache.

He watched for a repetition, but saw nothing.
He stared hard at the spot. The longer he looked,
the less certain he was he had seen anything. Then
he began to wonder whether he was looking at the
right place.

And it moved again. Something broke the light
for a moment. Where the moon had been rippling
on the surface there was a patch of darkness for a
moment. Then the moon was back. Forcing his
eyes wide, he stared hard at the spot. Shadows
from the willows and cottonwoods dappled the
glittering moonlight. Then he realized what he had
seen. Something had moved between two trees,
momentarily blocking the light, just long enough
for it to register.

Again, this time closer, the shade came and
went. Whoever it was was moving closer. Care-

fully, he stepped off the rock, gritting his teeth against the sudden cold. Still holding onto the branch, he moved forward a half-step, feeling the pressure of the sinewy limb lessen slightly. Another half-step and he could barely feel it. One more, and he could step away completely.

He moved forward, then knelt in the water, leaving just his head and shoulders out of the current. He knew the bulk of his body was disturbing the surface, forcing the swiftly moving water to swirl out and around, but if he stayed motionless, no one would notice, assuming it was either a rock or a tree-stump causing the deflection.

Leaning his cheek on the sandy strip, he sighted along the creek bank as far as he could. He heard nothing, but he knew someone was moving toward him. So far he didn't know how close to the creek they were, but guessed they would want to avoid the foliage as much as possible.

A high cloud crossed the moon and the bright surface of the creek disappeared. Shadows swallowed everything now, and Chance crawled out of the water, worming his way under the low-hanging willow branches. He banged his head on a large rock, suppressed a groan, and lay still for a long moment. He counted the seconds, and cursed when he got to thirty. At forty-five, it started to brighten again, and he realized he had been holding his breath the whole time.

Looking back toward the water now, he saw an unbroken seam of light. Anything that moved along his side of the creek would have to break the narrow band.

Something did.

At first he wasn't sure what it was. But it was definitely coming closer. Appearing and disappearing, then coming back again. Gradually, its shape refined, and he saw there were two. Feet, he realized. He was watching someone walk along the edge of the creek. Just as the realization hit him, he spotted a second pair, behind the first and closing in. As both pairs came closer, he caught more detail, the tell-tale rounded toe of Apache moccasins.

Could one of them be Lone Wolf? He wondered. Then realized he didn't have the luxury of waiting. If Lone Wolf were in the lead, then the warrior was stalking him. But suppose the stalker were Lone Wolf? How could he tell? What the hell should he do?

And suppose it was two warriors?

The possibilities swirled in his head like leaves in a flood, turning over and over too rapidly for him to focus on any one of them. He started to move, then stopped. He didn't know what to do. Then something broke the band of illumination further down the creek. He was prepared for it now, and knew right away it was another man, also an Apache. He was closing rapidly. An instant later, the second man caught the first.

He heard a gurgle, like the one he'd heard before. Then, without a sound, a lump of shadow descended on the creek bank. For a brief moment, as the body was lowered to the ground, he caught a glimpse of the face. It wasn't Lone Wolf.

He started to move as the third man picked up his pace, the feet rising and falling without a sound, narrowing the gap between himself and the man who had to be Lone Wolf. Chance exploded through the foliage, shouting at the same instant the warrior charged.

Chance broke into the open, lost his footing for a second and stumbled into the water. He saw the warrior raise his gun as he brought his own to bear. Lone Wolf was turning when both guns went off, Chance's just a split second sooner.

The charging warrior stopped, staggered for a second and fell headlong into the creek. The bullet had thrown his aim off just enough. Lone Wolf groaned and Chance scrambled to his feet. He waded through the fast moving current as Lone Wolf sat down heavily, blood streaming from his side.

The Apache held up a hand, shaking his head. "A graze," he said, gritting his teeth.

Chance took a normal breath for the first time since waking up. He wondered how much closer they could come. He knew the answer.

And he didn't want to think about it.

18

AT SUNUP, CHANCE BUILT A FIRE. This time, as he
struck the match, Lone Wolf smiled. "Okay," he said.

They ate quickly, without conversation. When
they were finished, Chance rolled a cigarette. He
offered the makings to the Apache, who shook his
head.

When he lit up, Chance exhaled a long, thin
stream of smoke. "What now?" he asked.

"Last night, I hear them talking. It is as I
thought. Juh is headed for Mexico, the Sierra
Madre."

"How far away is he now?"

"Not far. In Cold Canyon. He waits for the
army there."

"Why not just run for it? He's so far ahead, he
can make it easily."

"Some of his people want to go back. They say

there are worse things than bad beef and not enough of it. They say they should go back to the reservation. Juh tries to make them go with him, but so far they refuse."

"What does that mean, exactly? To us? Will they all fight?"

"If we attack before they separate, yes. If we wait, no."

"But if we wait, the army will catch up."

"Maybe."

"What do we do?" Chance didn't like asking advice. He felt like a child, and he was embarrassed to show his indecision to the Apache. But he was paralyzed. The cold hatred in his gut was still there, but he now knew it was not enough. It was fuel for what he had to do, but no more. Blind rage would get him killed, and then who would be left to avenge his family?

"Did they say anything about Wiley?" Chance asked.

Lone Wolf was quiet a long time. He scratched at the ground with a stick, sometimes making lines, sometimes just jabbing the dry wood into the drier soil. The Apache stood up and moved away. Chance thought he was not going to get an answer. But he was wrong.

"They meet Wiley at the other end of Cold Canyon. He has ammunition for them, and more guns."

"Could he be that stupid after what happened to the others, the wagon men?"

"Is Juh stupid to trust that it is not a trap?"

"I see your point."

Lone Wolf saddled his pony without saying another word. Chance, not knowing what else to do, followed suit. When they were ready, Lone Wolf took the lead. "Where are we going?" Chance asked.

"To find Juh."

They rode hard, pushing the horses just hard enough to make good time, not enough to exhaust them. Chance wanted to stop for lunch, but Lone Wolf refused. He ate in the saddle, and Chance had no choice but to down some more of the stringy venison, washing it down with tepid water from his canteen. As they moved south, the terrain got more barren. Less and less green dotted the flats and most of what there was was cactus.

By midafternoon, Lone Wolf picked up his pace a bit, angling toward the foot of a huge red mesa. It sat on the sandy bottom like a stranded ship, rusty and desolate, the highest thing for miles, and the only relief in the vast expanse. They reached the foot of the mesa just before sundown.

When Lone Wolf reined in, Chance understood why they had come this way. A small spring, little more than six feet across, ringed with green unlike anything they'd seen for thirty miles, sat placidly against the base of the sheer rock wall.

The Apache dismounted and dropped into a crouch. Moving forward in a stiff-legged strut without straightening, he shifted his body to let the fading sun highlight the ground. He nodded, pointing with a finger. "Here," he said.

Chance didn't see anything. He slid out of the saddle and moved in behind the Indian. He still didn't see anything.

"What is it?" he asked.

"Here," Lone Wolf said again, this time with a hint of impatience.

Chance lay flat on the ground, tilting his head every which way. "I just see a few scratches. It's nothing."

"No. This is where they brushed tracks with a branch. See the round mark?"

It was barely discernible. "So?"

"He walked on his heels. Then wiped away everything. But not good enough."

"I suppose you can tell me who it was, too."

The Apache glared at him.

Chance apologized. He wanted to explain that he was amazed, but thought better of it. The Indian knew. That was enough.

"We stay here tonight," the Apache said.

"Shouldn't we keep going?"

"No." That seemed to end it. Chance was angry, but he didn't want to push it. He needed Lone Wolf and the Apache knew it. Then, as if realizing what Chance was thinking, Lone Wolf said, "Juh will not move until he meets the army. Better that we rest."

Chance spent a restless night, wondering what would become of him. He felt as if he were being consumed by his desire for revenge, but instead of trying to control it, he wallowed in it. He felt it scouring him, the way a white hot poker cleanses a wound. It was burning away everything that was not real, and the only real thing now was his thirst for blood.

For a long time he lay there staring at the place where Lone Wolf slept. The Apache was an enigma to him. He thought about the man, examining him from every angle, as if he were a jewel box with a secret latch. But Lone Wolf was seamless, a smooth, unmarked stone with no trace of anything that was not surface, and that surface resisted all scrutiny. Questions came and went, but they ran off, the way rain runs off a round, smooth stone. Gone almost before one realized it.

He knew it must cost the Apache something, pride, maybe, to be working with him, just as it cost Chance something to work with him. But he got something in exchange, something as elusive as the Apache himself. It was there and it was genuine, but he didn't understand it.

Still baffled, he slipped off to sleep. And when he awoke, the first hint of gray in the sky, he was baffled still. He saw Lone Wolf pick up a small rock and toss it into the air. The Indian nodded. Without acknowledging that Chance was up, he said, "Time to go."

Chance grumbled. "Why so early?"

"To reach Cold Canyon before the sun sets. Or else it takes another day. I don't want to wait."

Chance didn't argue.

They were back in the saddle before the thick taste of sleep was gone from his mouth and tongue. By sunrise, they had covered ten miles. The mesa was just a red memory over his shoulder. He had to look back to remember what it looked like. Stark against the purple smear of the edge of the world, it looked less imposing at this range.

And ahead, the first fold of the Dragoon Mountains emerged from the morning haze. As the sun climbed higher, the haze began to disappear and the mountains seemed to crawl toward them slowly, like a half-drowned sailor creeping out of the breakers. San Carlos and Fort Apache were a distant memory to the north. Bisbee was somewhere to the southwest and, beyond it, Fort Huachuca. Behind them, to the northeast, Fort Bowie was the nearest military post, but it was seventy miles away. They were in the heart of Chiricahua country, the place from which Juh had sprung, like Cochise and Mangas Coloradas before him. This was Ki-Lo-Tah's country. And Chance was an alien.

Chance searched the sky for some hint that Juh and his warriors were waiting. There was no smoke, but Juh was too smart for that anyway. But there was no unusual movement, no nervous birds, nothing at all to suggest that anything was alive in those hot, dead stones.

But there was something else out there between them and the mountains. It was just a vague stain on the pale expanse. Under the brilliant light, it seemed to float above the ground. Chance thought it might be a mirage. He used the field glasses to bring it into sharper relief, but it still looked like nothing he could recognize.

He pointed it out to Lone Wolf who grunted. Chance handed him the binoculars, and the Apache studied the stain for several minutes. Finally, handing them back, he said, "Wagons."

"Wiley?"

"No."

The wagons weren't moving, because there was no dust. And no one in their right mind would stop in the middle of nowhere for no reason.

Chance decided not to question the Apache further. They pushed on, aware that their water was running dangerously low. Lone Wolf had two skins, but both were almost empty. Chance's canteen, which held less, was long since dry. His mouth was getting pasty. He took a swallow from the leathery tasting water skin draped over his saddle, shook it, and put it back.

"We come to a spring soon," Lone Wolf said. Chance licked his lips. At least there was water up ahead.

A mile closer, the glasses proved the Apache right. Three wagons, one lying on its side, shimmered in the white heat. There was no sign of anything living. The horses were gone, and the wagons appeared to be deserted.

Chance studied them for a minute, straining to keep the glasses still while his horse moved steadily forward. The wagons were just two miles away now, plain even to the naked eye. Lone Wolf seemed uninterested, as if he didn't care what had brought the wagons to this pass, or as if he already knew.

At half a mile, it was clear the wagons had been deserted. Crates, most of them broken open, lay spilled beside the one overturned wagon. The other two sat on their wheels. No sand or dust had accumulated around them, so they had to be fairly recent. They were approaching at an angle, and Chance spotted grooves in the sandy soil, fairly recent ruts, as if the wagons had come by in the last day or two.

But what had happened?

As they drew close, Lone Wolf goaded his

mount and the thirsty horse spurted forward. Chance struggled to keep up, but his horse was exhausted. They should stop at the wagons and change mounts, he thought. He looked up at the sun, which seemed to fall toward him. His cheeks grew hot from the direct light, and he started to feel giddy, as if he were falling through space while standing still.

When Chance reached the wagons, Lone Wolf was already on the ground. The Apache walked behind the overturned wagon as Chance dismounted. There was a fluttering and a screech, and he knew right away what it was. The first buzzard rose in the air, its wings beating angrily.

Then Chance noticed the smell. Several more of the scavengers squawked and flapped, rising just out of Lone Wolf's reach as Chance moved behind the wagon. Chance wanted to vomit. The stench was overpowering. As the Indian clubbed at the birds with the butt of his rifle, one yanked its slick head, dripping gore, from the slit belly of a fat man who lay on his back.

Three more corpses, each already picked over, almost unrecognizable as human beings lay sprawled in death. Eyes missing, lips ripped away, the faces all but gone, their limbs sprawled obscenely, the corpses shimmied as the birds darted in and out refusing to give up the free meal and tearing at the ragged, already rotting flesh.

All the bodies had been stripped, and two showed evidence of having been mutilated. Both thighs were slit down the middle, from hip to knee, and the stomach from navel to breastbone. Even through the tears of the buzzards, the smooth edges of the parted skin were apparent.

"My God," Chance said. He turned away, fighting the churning in his gut. He ran from the wagons, ignoring Lone Wolf's call to come back. He didn't stop until he was two hundred yards away. He ripped at his face with clawed fingers, trying to scrape away the stench. But it stayed in the air, swirling around him.

Chance bent over at the waist and spewed his breakfast onto the sand.

He heard the Apache coming up behind him, and whirled. "How can you just stand there like nothing happened? What's wrong with you?"

"You were in the army?"

Chance nodded.

"Then you have seen this before. So have I."

"But . . ." Chance was speechless.

Lone Wolf held up an arrow and pointed to the distinctive winding near the head. "Juh," he said.

Chance nodded, then noticed the graying flesh still clinging to the arrowhead. He coughed and rubbed his palms against his cheeks. He gagged again, but there was nothing left to come up.

19

IT WAS NEAR SUNDOWN. The mouth of Cold Canyon yawned as wide as the gates of hell. In the dark blue swath of the Dragoon Mountains, it was a huge, darker spot. The declining ball of sun seemed to fall toward it, then disappeared by degrees, the way a rat slips down a serpent's maw.

Lone Wolf pulled up. He watched the sun slide all the way down, a sun dog glittering behind him for a few minutes then winking out. It got dark quickly, as if some one had closed a curtain in a tubercular's room.

Chance sat his horse quietly, waiting for the Apache to say something. Lone Wolf had been silent since they left the ruined wagons behind. Something about the massacre had changed him somehow. His whole manner had gotten chilly. If stone could have gotten harder, that's what had happend to the Indian.

His jaw, never loose as it was, locked like a vise, muscles bunched at the hinge of his jaw, twitching as he ground his teeth. There was a volcano inside him, Chance thought, and the lava was beginning to boil. Lone Wolf didn't want it to happen. He fought against it. But passion was winning out over his natural stoicism.

It was frightening to watch, and Chance unconsciously let his mount drift a little to the left and hang back a few lengths, as if the Apache were too hot a fire. He wanted to ask, but didn't dare.

They were both thirsty. Juh's people had poisoned the last waterhole, gutting a horse in the small pond, and leaving the carcass mired in the muddy bottom. Drinking was out of the question. Even boiling was risky. They had chosen to pass. There was abundant water in the heart of the canyon, where two springs filled a pool nearly fifty feet across. The water was clear, cold and, unlike most of the ground swells in this part of the wilderness, untainted by metal salts or alkali.

Thinking about it made the thirst worse. Not thinking about it was too big a lie for Chance to tell himself. He wanted a drink in the worst way. But if Lone Wolf was right, the canyon belonged to Juh. Getting to the springs would be worth his hide. But if you were thirsty enough, Chance thought, it was a small enough price to pay.

When the sun had been down for fifteen minutes, the last gold edges of the clouds were extinguished, turning the blue-black mass to the west a dark blue-gray. For a moment, blades of light speared out in every direction, palpable as swords. It was breathtaking, and Chance watched in awe until the darkness was complete.

Finally, suddenly, like a mission-bell at sunrise, Chance broke the silence. "Do you think they know we're here, Ki-Lo-Tah?" He surprised himself, using the Apache name.

Lone Wolf appeared not to notice. "They know."

The jaw snapped shut. There was no room for doubt, not now and certainly not here. Lone Wolf wouldn't permit it, and Chance was not inclined to want it. This close certainty was their only ally. Certainty and darkness, that surrounded them, and that deeper darkness inside them.

It was two miles to the mountains, and Lone Wolf slipped from his horse. He looped the reins of his mount to his left hand and started walking. In his right hand, he held a Winchester, its hammer cocked. Chance joined the Apache on the ground. The hollow clop-clop-clop of the sixteen hooves was muted by the sand. Chance listened to it, then tried to listen past it, focusing himself on the mountains, and the men who waited there to kill him if they could.

But he had to look beyond the mountains, too, to the last man, the one who lurked behind it all.

What was Tucker Wiley doing, he wondered. Did he know what had happened? Did he know Chance was coming for him?

But that was dangerous. He couldn't let himself look too far ahead. There was too much between him and Wiley. The potential for sudden death was too real for him to think about the future. For the next twenty-four hours, he could only afford to look ahead a second at a time, just enough to see the tautened bowstring or the cocked hammer. Look past it, and he was finished. Fail to look far enough ahead, and it would be on him too quickly for him to react.

For the moment, time was an incredibly fine wire, stretched between the immediate past and the imminent future. He had to watch where he was going, not worry about where he placed his feet. If he misstepped, fell somehow, the wire would cut him in two or it would break. Either way, it would mean disaster.

At one mile from the mouth of the canyon, Lone Wolf slowed, then finally halted. Chance stopped, maintaining the gap. The Apache was just far enough ahead to be a gray blur in the darkness, not far enough that Chance would lose sight of him. He turned, came back toward Chance, something dangling from his fist.

"Take off your boots," he said.

"What?"

"Your boots. Take them off."

"Why?"

"Do it . . ."

Chance sat on the ground and tugged at his boots, struggling to get them free. When both were off, Lone Wolf dropped something in his lap. It smelled of newness, and he had to hold it close to see what it was. The smell was leather. It was a pair of moccasins.

Apache style.

Chance looked at the Indian, but Lone Wolf's face was almost obscured, hovering above him as ill-defined as a cloud. He tugged one of the moccasins on, stretched his leg and bent it under him. Pulling on the second, he admired the way it slid up along his calf like a second skin under the legs of his dungarees.

"Where did you . . . ?"

"Let's go."

They closed on the canyon mouth slowly. Even in the darkness, it was blacker still. Just inside the opening, stunted trees, shielded by the rock from the worst of the sun, but twisted by the lack of water, formed a tangled curtain. Lone Wolf led the horses in. He was perfectly quiet. Chance could hear his own breathing and nothing else.

Lone Wolf was back a moment later. The water-skins dangled from one fist. The Winchester, still cocked, was gripped firmly in the other.

"Stay here," he said.

"Where are you . . ."

The Apache held up the skins. "We need water."

"We can both go."

"No."

And he vanished. Chance marvelled at the speed which made no sound. One second Lone Wolf was standing in front of him. The next, he was gone. Chance fought the urge to go after him. He sat on the ground to stop his head from spinning. Juh was out there, with nearly a dozen men, and this was his country, his and Lone Wolf's. Chance did not belong.

Tomorrow, he thought, when the sun comes up, the deck will not be so unevenly stacked.

Or would it?

The Apache was gone for over an hour. In his mind, Chance tried to sketch a map of the canyon. He'd been through it only twice, once in each direction. He had then the vague sensation of crawling through the entrails of a rattler that had been flayed and laid open to the sky, its backbone removed to admit the light of day.

Sheer walls, more than two hundred feet high in some places, wound for more than a mile, coiling back on themselves more than once. Less than a quarter-mile wide at its widest, it was tailor made for an ambush, and it was the only way through the Dragoon Mountains for ten miles in either direction.

Juh had to know that Crook would know this.

His decision to stand and fight at the most obvious place was a calculated insult. And a challenge. It suggested that Juh was prepared to die, but only on his terms, and only at his price, which would be high.

And behind him, Chance felt an invisible pressure. It was almost as if the air pushed ahead of itself by the mounted column that had to be coming, was building up. Chance was in the way, a small cork in a bottle-neck. He was inconsequential. To Juh, he was probably a joke, a single sandfly to be swatted without a second thought. To the army, at best, he was a fool who would almost certainly get himself killed and at worst he was a fugitive, interfering where he should not.

He imagined Crook peering at him over his reading glasses, not even bothering to ask him why. The old general would just shake his head, a wise man confronted by the village idiot.

He was nearly asleep when the Apache returned. He felt embarrassed, then realized Lone Wolf had probably expected no more of him anyway. The Indian tossed him a skin. He popped the wooden plug and drank greedily, ashamed of himself but too thirsty to care. When he had drunk his fill, he asked, "Is he here?"

Lone Wolf nodded.

The moon came up then, and Chance saw blood on the Apache's shirt. So, he thought, the water came with a price. He wanted to ask, but knew the Apache would say nothing. As if he didn't even wish to hear the question, Lone Wolf backed into the shadow of the canyon wall. Even in the moon's full light, Chance couldn't see him.

But he was, finally and whole-heartedly, glad he was there.

20

AT DAWN, LONE WOLF handed Chance a water-skin. From the saddlebags on his follow horse he pulled two more cartridge belts, draped one over his blue blouse Mexican style, and buckled it. He handed the other to Chance.

"Juh will be high up," the Apache said. "We have to get higher."

Chance buckled the cartridge belt around his waist. He nodded. Lone Wolf led the way. Climbing through a tangle of boulders, Chance was struck by the maze-like approach. Flutes and chimneys of rock sprang out of the ground like the trunks of enormous trees. Walls like flying buttresses swept down and away from the sheer rock face. Twice, he stumbled into blind alleys.

The Apache moved so quietly, when he turned a corner, or dropped out of sight below a boulder,

Chance was afraid he might lose him. The Indian walked on his heels, leaving strange, rounded impressions on the bone-dry layer of dust and sand.

The ground fell away behind them, and as he looked back, he started to get nauseous. Lone Wolf found handholds in the rock and dragged himself full length up twelve and fifteen foot high walls. He found a way to climb when Chance thought the rock wall was as smooth as a mirror.

Unused to the thin leather soles of the moccasins, Chance found the going rough. Not accustomed to placing his feet as carefully as the Apache, he kept stepping on sharp edges that made him grit his teeth to keep from crying out.

Rounding a huge slab of stone, he felt a hand grab him by the arm and pull him down. A second later, an Apache appeared from behind a chimney rock. The Indian listened for a moment, then crouched down and duck-walked to a nearby boulder. Lone Wolf leaned close to whisper, "Wait here."

A second later, he was gone. Chance felt the sweat on his palms begin to flow. He gun was slippery, and he dried first one hand then the other on the sand. Taking another handful of the powdery silt, he wiped the grip down, careful not to get any of the dirt in the mechanism.

Something moved off to the right. Lone Wolf, a thick-bladed knife in his left hand, crept behind the chimney the hostile had just left. A second later, in a blur of limbs, he charged behind the rock. Something thumped and Chance darted forward. He charged around the rock as Lone Wolf lowered the sentry to the ground. One hand was clamped over the guard's mouth, the other out of sight until the Indian lay quivering on the ground. Only when the spastic limbs stopped moving did Lone Wolf uncover the Indian's mouth. He jerked the hidden hand free, wiped the bloody blade on the dead man's shirt and stuck the knife back in its sheath.

Chance allowed himself to breathe again. He stared down at the corpse, wondering if this was the man who had killed Jenny, then decided he would rather not know. Besides, he told himself, the Indian, whichever one it was, had just been the instrument. The man responsible was Tucker Wiley. And that was one corpse he would be glad to see. Imperceptibly, he realized, he was coming around to Lone Wolf's point of view. Chasing Juh was chasing the dog's tail. Wiley was the dog's head. It was the head he wanted. It was the head he should cut off.

And would.

The sun was behind them, and he could feel its heat on his back as he climbed. He was grateful, without really thinking much about it, that the sun wasn't in his eyes. The going was treacherous enough without having an additional handicap.

Looking back down the path they had come, Chance guessed they were more than a hundred feet in the air.

The trail was anything but direct, but Lone Wolf showed no signs of tiring. He moved as swiftly and silently now as he had at the bottom. Chance was having a hard time breathing. His tongue felt thick in his throat, and his knees felt as if they had been dipped in molten lead. Every bend sent a sheet of flame spurting up the front of his thighs.

There was still more than a hundred vertical feet to go, and God knew how many hundreds of steps. He doubled over, resting his weight on bent knees and gasped for air. Lone Wolf stared back down the trail at him, his face a mixture of pity and impatience.

Chance waved a feeble hand at him, telling him to go on, but the Apache stayed rooted to the spot. Whether the Indian was humoring him, or whether he truly needed him, Chance couldn't decide. But he didn't figure on being much use once he managed to get up top. If he managed it at all.

He straightened up, flexed his knees a couple of times and winced at the pain. His feet felt as if someone had peeled the soles away and left him walking on the ends of bloody bones. Every step was agony.

Finally, Lone Wolf moved on, vanishing behind a huge slab of rock angled against the face of the mountain. The slab looked as if the least breeze would dislodge it. Lone Wolf had ducked into a natural cave under the rock, and yanked Chance by the sleeve as he went by.

The Apache slipped out of the crevice and shoved Chance in.

"Wait here," he said.

"But . . ."

"I'll be right back."

Chance was too grateful for the reprieve to argue. He watched the Apache go, and realized he had been holding him back. On the trail it was one thing, but now, when sudden death could be hiding behind any rock, it was far more serious. Chance massaged his aching knees, trying to ease the pain. He took a swig of water, spat it out, then took a mouthful and swallowed it.

The water refreshed him, but he had to fight the urge to drink more. Better to know it was there on his hip than drink it all now and not know when he'd get another swig.

The pain subsided a little, and his breathing became easier. He lay there under the huge stone, thinking that if it shifted a little, it could become at once the instrument of his death and his mausoleum. He shrugged it off. Death was no longer intimidating. And at least that one would be sudden, total and relatively painless, squashed like a bug.

He heard something then. Just a whisper, like cloth rubbing against stone. He held his breath straining for a repetition. Instead, a shadow spilled over the opening. It was someone coming up the trail. Not Lone Wolf, who had gone higher. The figure moved again, this time etching itself on the sand in profile. Long locks, held back on the sides, falling to the shoulders, then a rifle barrel, all shadow.

He shifted his position, moving the Winchester so slowly he thought it would never come around. The shadow moved again, and he saw a moccasined foot, not five feet from where he sat.

The Apache moved then, darting up the trail several feet. Chance drew a bead, then realized he couldn't shoot without exposing their presence, and possibly getting Lone Wolf in a jam.

Cautiously, he gathered his legs beneath him. At the first sound, the Indian would turn, and there was no reason for him not to shoot. Chance bulled forward. The Apache heard his first step and started to turn as Chance hit him. Driving his shoulder into the small of the Apache's back, they crashed into the rock. The Indian's rifle skittered away, sliding on the sandy slope. The man was small, but he was powerful, thick arms pushing them both up and away from the ground as Chance struggled to hold on.

He got the rifle around and under the Apache's

chin and yanked it back hard. Letting the Winchester slide to both elbows, he locked it against the Apache's throat and bent his arms back. The man started to gag as Chance lifted him off the ground. Chance locked his hands behind his head and bent backward.

Something snapped, and the Apache shivered once. The stench of voided bowels swirled around them and Chance shook the warrior like a terrier with a rat, just to make sure. He dropped the body and backed away, stunned by his own violence. He stood there shaking, the adrenaline coursing through his veins making his heart hammer at his ribs like an angry fist. He saw the Apache's gun, started to run for it, then remembered where he was . . . and why. Chance dropped into a crouch and peered out around the redstone slab. The trail leading down was deserted.

He looked up, thought he saw something, and ducked out of sight. He had to do something with the body, and gnawed his lip while he tried to decide. Not knowing what else to do, he grabbed the Apache under the arms and dragged him toward the crevice. The man was heavier than he looked, all bone and muscle.

Chance tried to shove the corpse in under the rock, but it wouldn't go. Holding his breath, he squeezed past, then dragged the man by his arms until he was out of sight from the trail. Squeezing back over the body, face to face for a moment, he thought he saw the eyes blink. He swallowed hard and waited. A fly, already drawn by the smell of death, landed on the Apache's cheek. It crawled up toward the eye, then over the nose. The Indian never moved. As an afterthought, he grabbed the Apache's pistol, a brand new Colt, and tucked it into his belt.

Breathing a sigh of relief, Chance hauled himself out of the crevice. He crawled downhill feet first, his eyes on the rocks above him, alert for the slightest motion, until he felt the rifle against his shin. He pinned it to the ground, slid down another two feet until he could reach it with his free hand, and tugged it toward him.

With the rifle in tow, he crawled back to cover and lay there panting. Looking back down, he saw the wide swath of scuff marks on the trail, the impressions made by his knees and the heels of his hands, the deep gouge made by his belt buckle. They were a dead giveaway, but there was nothing he could do about it.

Where the hell was Lone Wolf, he wondered, almost saying it out loud.

He was going to have to get over the jitters. If he wanted to come out of this alive, he couldn't afford to be his own worst enemy. Sucking in the hot dry air, the musty smell of the dust filled his nostrils and, underneath it, the thick, fetid stink of the dead man.

"Easy," he whispered, "take it easy, Dalton. You'll be alright." And he was starting to believe it. He crawled up the face of the red slab and lay there for a long time, watching the wall across the canyon. Like this side, it was networked with trails and alleyways. He tried to focus on them one by one, but the strain was killing him. And he kept teasing himself that while he was watching one spot, Juh and his warriors were crawling all over, just beyond the edge of his attention.

He took a deep breath, held it a moment, then let it out slowly. It was time to try a different approach. He opened his eyes wide, trying to look at nothing in particular, waiting instead for something to move, to draw him to it.

Absorbed in his surveillance, he nearly screamed when he felt a hand close over his ankle. He turned around, bringing the rifle around as a club at the same instant. He arrested the rifle in mid-swing when he realized the hand belonged to his one ally on the mountain.

Lone Wolf held a finger to his lips and backed down the rock. Chance felt like an idiot. Just when he was starting to congratulate himself for mastering the skills he'd need to survive, he let a man come within an arm's length of him without even realizing he was there.

He backed down the rock and Lone Wolf pulled him in under the overhang. If he noticed the body stuffed into the back of the crevice, he didn't let on.

"Four this side. Six that side," he said. "All higher."

"You mean we have to go all the way up?" His joints screamed as he asked the question. The Apache nodded.

"From the top, we can shoot down at them. If we attack from below, they will win."

"Can we win, even if we get above them?"

The Apache shrugged. "*Quien sabe,*" he said.

Chance was quiet. He thought about the last few days and tried to piece them together in some meaningful sequence, but all he could get was fragments. Little scraps came back to him, in no order, one unconnected from the other. He wondered whether there was any point in praying, just in case. He nodded. "Alright then," he said. "Let's go."

It took more than an hour to make it to the top. Lone Wolf, with a better idea of the deployment Juh had chosen, concentrated on the climb, taking a roundabout route, but one that let him move quickly, unconcerned with discovery. Chance seemed to have tapped new reserves of energy. He kept pace, his knees no longer screaming. They still hurt, but he was able to brush the pain aside. One step at a time, he told himself, just one step at a time.

It was high noon as they neared the rim of the high wall. Chance hauled himself up the last ten feet and lay there on his stomach, his ribs heaving as he tried to regain his equilibrium.

He looked up at the sun, squinting against the glare. Slowly, his heart stopped hammering against his aching ribs. It was time. He climbed wearily to his feet.

There was no turning back now.

21

THE TOP OF THE MOUNTAIN was almost table-like. Littered with boulders, it stretched ahead for nearly a mile, slowly rising in a modest slope to a rounded hilltop. It was is if they were on a different floor of the world. Lone Wolf squatted on his haunches and drew his knife. With a flick of his wrist, he carved a replica of the canyon's meandering contours with the top of his blade, holding it perpendicular to the direction of the line to make it broad enough to show some detail.

Using pebbles as markers, he quickly placed all ten of Juh's band, reserving the largest stone for the chief himself. "They are set up to push rocks down on the column when it comes," he said. "If I am here, and you here," punctuating each "here" with the point of the blade, he indicated a large, squarish boulder on the rimrock for his location, and a twisted mesquite bush for Chance's, "we can each see two men on our side. When you are in position and you see your two men, raise your hand. I will do the same. Only then do we shoot. Are you a good shot?" Lone Wolf glanced at his face, as if to make sure Chance told him the truth.

Chance nodded. "Very good. But it's been awhile."

"No time for practice," Lone Wolf said, with no trace of a smile.

"What about those on the other side?"

"There will be a sentry, like on this side. He will be too far down to be a problem. Another warrior will move from place to place, like the man you killed."

"You saw him?"

Lone Wolf nodded, pointed to the Colt in Chance's belt, then continued. "I know some of them. They are good shots, but not at this range."

"Where's Juh?" Chance asked, then said "oh," when he remembered. He was across the canyon. Chance was sorry he wouldn't get to shoot at him now, thinking that killing the chief might break the back of the renegades' determination.

"They will come to us," Lone Wolf said. "If we get those on this side."

"And if we don't?"

"They won't have to." So, there it was. So simple, so damned matter of fact. Lone Wolf was con-

ceding the field, unless the surgical assault was immediately successful. "We can miss one, but only
one," he said. Again he glanced at Chance, to
make sure the point had registered. When he was
satisfied, he said, "If you have any questions,
Chance, now is the time to ask. Otherwise . . ."

"Let's go," Chance said. He didn't want time to
think about it.

Lone Wolf headed toward his position, drop-
ping to his stomach when he was still fifty feet
from the edge. Chance sprinted toward the
mesquite, dropped to his knees a good thirty yards
in front of it, and crawled the rest of the way.
Crouching beside a flat rock, he raised his head
just enough to see over the lip of the canyon. He
spotted the first warrior immediately. Like most
Apaches, he hadn't worried about color giving him
away. Adept at hiding above the enemy, they didn't
bother with protective coloration or camouflage
when it wasn't necessary.

The second man was a little harder to find.
Chance glanced toward Lone Wolf, saw the
Apache raise his hand, then looked back at the
sloping canyon wall. A narrow ledge, its edge lined
with rocks on the canyon side, snaked along the
wall some two hundred yards in either direction.
His first man was almost directly below him. The
other had to be somewhere in that narrow strip.

A moment later, he spotted him, crouched between two large rocks. The warrior was almost hidden by the boulders. Chance would get only one shot, and it better be good. He checked the first man again, checked the cover available to him in either direction. There wasn't much. If he nailed the more distant man, he'd have several seconds to lever another round, sight, and get off his second shot.

It would be close timing, but there was no other way.

He raised his hand. Sighting in on the first target, he aimed carefully. Shooting down was one of the most difficult shots, because the bullet tended to drop anyway, and it was easy to undershoot. He compensated slightly, aiming a little high, but not so much as to overshoot. He had a range of six or eight inches. Dead center would probably be too low.

Ready as he would ever be, he watched Lone Wolf for a signal. When it came, he squeezed, not even hearing the report as he swung his Winchester around. The second man was already moving, glancing up as he sprinted away. Chance found him over the sight, led him a little and squeezed. The shot went wide and the warrior dove for cover. Jerking another shell into the chamber, Chance resighted. The Apache was scrambling on all fours as Chance squeezed.

The carbine bucked, but he saw a bright red

geyser high on the Apache's back, just under the collarbone. Levering again, he sighted in and fired. He caught the warrior just a foot from cover. The man sprawled headlong, then tried to haul himself by brute force behind a jumble of rocks.

Chance backed away as a bullet slammed into the mesquite bush, clipping leaves and snapping off a small branch. It took him several seconds to realize the Apaches across the canyon were firing at him.

He looked toward Lone Wolf as he hugged the ground. Shot after shot chipped at the rocks ahead of him, shredded through the mesquite like a thresher, and whistled off into the bright blue sky.

Lone Wolf raised a hand, then started backing away from the edge of the canyon. Chance did likewise.

"They shoot many bullets. That means they have many. Or they are expecting to get more," Lone Wolf said, when Chance was close enough to hear him. The firing slacked off, then stopped altogther.

"That means they're expecting Wiley, doesn't it?" Chance asked.

The Indian shook his head. "Yes."

"What now?"

Lone Wolf got to his feet and looked at the sun. It was past noon, but there was still plenty of daylight left. He looked toward the ragged edge of the canyon, as if trying to decide something, then said, "They will come to us."

"Are you sure?"

He nodded.

The plateau stretched out behind them and ahead lay the canyon, like a tear in the earth through which something terrible would come. Chance knew the Apaches had the advantage. There were still six of them, and almost unlimited options. They could come up the face of the canyon, or they could use one of several trails. They might come in a group, or they might spread out, and pick their way, one at a time.

There was also the chance, although remote, that some of them would choose not to come at all. Unlike some tribes, the Apaches did not follow a leader because they had to. They followed because they wanted to, or they didn't follow at all. Even Geronimo was supposed to have changed his plans more than once when some of his warriors disagreed with him.

The advantage of surprise was gone now. Juh knew they were there, and he probably knew it was just the two of them. Whether he chose to overwhelm them in a quick, furious assault or wait for dark and try to take them by surprise was anybody's guess. Or Lone Wolf's. Certainly Chance would not attempt to predict what Juh would do.

Lone Wolf sat down, bent his legs underneath

him, and lay his Winchester across his lap. He watched the canyon rim with one eye while reloading the carbine's magazine. When he was finished, he nodded that Chance should reload his own weapon.

As each shell clicked home, the sharp, metallic sound reinforced the deathly silence. When he was done, the quiet was complete. A sudden shriek caused him to look up. A huge hawk, its giant wings motionless, spiralled down in a broad, gentle sweep. With a second cry, the bird folded its wings and fell like a stone.

Then, with the sharp crack of canvas hitting a stiff wind, the great wings unfolded as the hawk softened its dive, clawed at something scurrying across the plateau, then climbed. Whatever it was twisted and turned in the talons, its shrill cries growing more and more feeble until they died away altogether. The returning silence seemed all the deeper for the brief interruption.

Chance turned away from the bird to look at the Apache. Lone Wolf, too, had been watching the hawk. When he felt Chance staring at him, he turned away. Quietly, he stood and backed away from the rim even further. Chance watched, wondering whether the Apache wanted to be alone, or if he were suddenly aware of something about to happen.

Chance started to move and Lone Wolf dropped

to his stomach, shoved his carbine out ahead of him and propped himself up on his elbows. He stared past Chance, his eyes immobile, maybe not even blinking, Chance wasn't sure.

"Are they coming?" he asked.

"Not yet."

"Then why are . . ."

Lone Wolf held up a hand. He shook his head from side to side, a negative addressed, apparently, to the unspoken end of Chance's question.

Chance sat down, his hands in his lap, his Winchester bridging his knees. He fiddled with the lever, wiped his palms on his pants, picked up a pebble and rolled it thoughtfully in his fingers. He let the stone roll into his palm. His skin was torn and rubbed raw in some places. Against the ripped flesh, the stone seemed so permanent, invulnerable, and made the flesh that held it look feeble.

He heard something, a scraping sound, then a rock fell away from the edge of the canyon. He tucked the pebble into his pocket, and brought the rifle to his shoulder. Sweeping the rim from left to right, he traced the jagged line with the gunsight. He forced his eyes to open wide, despite the brilliant sun. Again, a noise, and he jerked his head to the left, certain that someone was about to climb up and over the rimrock.

But nothing happened.

He spat, found his mouth too dry, and licked his

lips with a tongue that felt like it was made of old leather. He wanted a drink. He wanted to lie back and go to sleep. His nerves were too tight. The least little thing might snap them, and he was afraid of what he would do then.

For a moment, he wanted to get up and walk to the edge of the canyon. He started to get up, when he heard another scrape.

"They are here," Lone Wolf said. Chance swivelled his head from side to side, the gun growing heavy in his hands. His back ached with the strain of constant alertness. He felt as if he were starting to collapse in on himself, maybe curling into a ball against his will, like an armadillo trying to protect itself. He wanted to scream. His mouth opened, but the words wouldn't come.

The scraping grew louder, and it confused him. Why would the Apaches make so much noise? Was it some kind of trick? He looked at Lone Wolf, who seemed just as baffled. It was almost as if the noise were deliberate, some kind of announcement, but of what?

And then he saw it, suddenly swept into view over the rimrock.

A white flag.

22

CHANCE FELT HIS FINGER HESITATE. The Apache climbed over the canyon rim, waving the white flag awkwardly in one hand. The Indian looked at Chance, slowly straightened up and raised his free hand. He stood there on the very lip of the canyon. Chance wondered what would happen if he pulled the trigger. Would the Apache just tumble backward and disappear?

Holding the rifle steady, he became conscious of the strain, his body starting to tremble. The iron sight wavered, and he couldn't bring it back on target. He squeezed. The rifle cracked, but the shot went high and to the left.

Chance heard footsteps behind him. He dropped the rifle and covered his face with his hands. Lone Wolf rushed past him and when he looked up, the scout was hauling the Apache back up over the canyon's edge. Chance didn't know whether the warrior had fallen, tried to climb back down, or if he had simply been frightened and seeking cover.

The white flag, a simple strip of cotton tied to a gnarled stick, lay on the ground. Chance looked at it instead of the Indians. He was ashamed and angry. Angry at himself, partly, and furious at the presumption of the Apache, thinking that two cents worth of ragged cotton could protect him from the rage Chance felt boiling inside him.

He reached for his Winchester again, tried to sight in on Juh's warrior, then realized he hadn't ejected the spent cartridge. He jerked the lever. Lone Wolf heard the click and turned. The scout almost lost his grip on the warrior as he raised one hand toward Chance.

Chance brought the warrior back into his sights. His hands were trembling and he wanted to pull the trigger almost as much as he wanted Jenny back. And that was the thought that broke his resolve. He could pull the trigger till Doomsday, if he wanted. But Jenny was never coming back. Jenny was dead. The boys were dead. And in front of him was one of the men who had helped to kill them.

He let his breath out in a long, trembling sigh. It was surrender to the irreversible. And if the white flag meant nothing to him, he was no better than the savage in his sights.

Chance lowered the carbine, let it slip from his fingers. He stood and walked slowly toward the two Apaches. They had stopped struggling now, and Lone Wolf gave him a long look as Chance approached to within ten feet and stopped.

"Tell him I'm sorry," Chance said.

"Are you?" Lone Wolf gave him a searching look.

"I guess not."

That seemed to satisfy the scout. He said something to the warrior, then waited for a response. It was a long time in coming. A sharp crack broke the stillness. The bullet whistled high and to the right, but both Indians dropped to the ground. Chance stood there watching them as if he were unaware.

"Get down," Lone Wolf shouted.

Chance just looked at him.

"Get down, Chance," the scout said again.

Chance backed up three or four steps, but stayed on his feet. "Ask him what he wants," he said.

"What do you think he wants? Doesn't that flag tell you what he wants?"

Chance laughed. It was a bitter sound, more than a little incredulous. He felt it in his throat like he were disgorging a woodrasp. "Surrender?" Chance shook his head. "He wants to surrender, doesn't he." This time it wasn't a question.

Lone Wolf said something in Apache. The warrior responded, then looked at Chance while he waited for Lone Wolf to translate.

"He says he and another man want to surrender."

"Ask him why."

Again there was a pause while the two Apaches conversed in the strange language whose sounds were as harsh as the landscape from which they sprang.

"He says they don't want to fight for Juh anymore. He says Juh is crazy and will get them all killed. He says Pionsonnay has gone back to San Carlos already to turn himself in. He says the army is coming, and he doesn't want to die."

"Nobody wants to die," Chance said. "Jenny didn't want to die. My boys didn't want to die. You tell him that."

Lone Wolf said nothing.

"Go on," Chance shouted. "Tell him that. You tell that red bastard my wife didn't want to die and I didn't want her to die and my boys didn't want to die. They wanted to live and it didn't save them. And I want *him* to die, and nothing on this earth will save him. You tell him that! Go on . . ."

Lone Wolf started to translate and Chance, knowing what he was saying, couldn't bear to listen, even though he didn't understand a word of the language. He turned his back and walked away. He saw his rifle lying on the ground where he had left it. He walked over and stood over it, staring down at the weapon as if it were something he had never seen before. Slowly, he leaned forward and picked it up.

Chance turned back to the Apaches. He raised the rifle and sighted in again. The Apache warrior stared back at him, but didn't flinch. He said something to Lone Wolf. Lone Wolf nodded, and looked at Chance, but didn't translate.

"What did he say?" Chance asked.

"It doesn't matter."

"Is that what he said? Or are you telling me that what he said doesn't matter?"

"Both."

Chance found the trigger. He squeezed. The Winchester bucked. The Apache stared down at the gouged earth between his feet for a moment, then slowly raised his head. Again he said something which Lone Wolf didn't translate.

"What'd he say, dammit?" Chance levered another shell home.

"He says he understands how you feel. He says he has lost family to the white man. A wife, a mother and father, three children. He says he would die to bring them back if he could, but he can't, so what happens to him doesn't make any difference."

"Ask him who killed my family."

Lone Wolf translated the question, then took a

deep breath. The scout listened carefully to the answer. Chance also listened, trying to decide what the answer would be.

When the Apache fell silent, Lone Wolf translated immediately. "Juh and another Apache. The other man is dead."

"Do you know who it was? Did he say?"

"He said, yes."

"Did I . . ."

Lone Wolf nodded. "Josanie. The man on the trail."

"You're sure?"

Again, the scout nodded. "Yes. I am sure."

Chance sighed. He uncocked the carbine, lowered it, and walked toward the Apaches.

Lone Wolf said, "Juh will come after us soon. He knows the army is coming. He can't wait, because he will be trapped here."

"Let him come," Chance said. He walked to the rim of the canyon, not even bothering to crouch. He looked down into the yawning seam in the earth as if expecting to see Juh himself staring up at him. But the canyon was deserted, a great, meandering seam that had sprung its stitches, the earth parting like cheap cloth. He could see the boulders littering the canyon floor, partly in shadow. The sheer wall of the far side fell straight down, more than two hundred feet. It was formidable, but not for the Apaches.

Chance backed away, still staring into the chasm, unable to take his eyes off it. Over his shoulder, he said, "Which way will he come?"

"I don't know," Lone Wolf said.

"How about your friend? Does he have any idea?"

"He says not."

"You believe him?"

"Yes."

"Then I guess we just sit here and wait."

"There is nothing else we can do. If we go down, he will know, and he will stay where he is. He will have the advantage."

"But we are no threat to him here, and he knows it."

"We have time. Juh has no time."

So they waited.

Chance sat on the ground, just behind a cluster of small, rounded stones. There wasn't much cover up top, and the two Apaches made do with similar piles of rock. Chance became conscious of the sun pressing down on him. He didn't like being on the defensive, but the truth was, there was no way they could bring the fight to Juh. They were on his home ground, and the initiative was his.

Chance wanted to string the three of them out like pickets along the rimrock, but Lone Wolf refused. He argued they would be trapped close to the rim and that it was better to be able to move in any direction, even if it meant giving Juh unopposed access to the top of the plateau. "Better," the Apache argued, "to fight on open ground."

Chance was reluctant at first. But he was an interloper, Lone Wolf and the other Apache, whose Spanish name was Juanito, were worse. They were turncoats. Things would go very badly with them if Juh should win. They seemed not to be frightened of the prospect. The odds were better now, five to three, and just maybe, Chance thought, we can pull it off.

He was getting impatient, and he struggled against the urge to do something precipitous. Juh was counting on that nervousness, hoping he would do something stupid. Well, Juh could guess again.

When the attack finally came, Chance was mometarily stunned, as if he had forgotten why he was waiting there in the first place. They came from all sides, arrayed along the canyon for three hundred yards in every direction.

The first shot came from the left. Chance swung his carbine toward the sound, and another shot, this one from the far right, jerked him in the opposite direction. Then all five were firing at once.

Chance got on his stomach and kept his eyes on the canyon rim. The Apaches were firing at will, one popping up as another ducked. It was impossible to draw a bead. They moved too quickly.

Charging the rim was out of the question. There was virtually no cover between the little jumble of rocks and the edge of the canyon. The only thing to do was back up. Maybe it would draw them out.

And maybe not.

Chance shouted to Lone Wolf, then started to creep backward, his nose dragging in the parched earth. It was awkward, but he didn't dare take his eyes off the rimrock. Bullets sailed over his head from every direction. The repeated cracks of the Apache rifles, first the middle, then the left, then somewhere in between, then the right and back to the middle, had him quaking. His spine felt as if it had been encased in ice.

Behind him, fifty or sixty feet away, another rock, this one solitary, stuck up out of the ground as if it had been planted by a giant hand. Chance kept backpedaling until his feet slammed into the rock.

He was exposed to fire from the left and rolled quickly right, scrambling behind the rock just ahead of a fusillade chiseling at the boulder like an angry sculptor. Chips of stone nicked the exposed skin of his neck and arms, one sliver embedding itself in the flesh of his shoulder.

He ripped it out, looked at it curiously, then tossed it aside. He felt only a thin trickle of blood under his shirt sleeve.

Lone Wolf had been watching him. He and the defector had fired sporadically, enough to keep the Apaches guessing but not enough to do any real damage.

Ensconced behind the boulder, he felt no less frightened. Tremors shook his upper body, and his legs were made of gelatin. But the rock was larger and he could kneel now, use the rock as a firing platform as well as cover.

The defector jumped to his feet and backpedaled now, heading toward a tangle of mesquite and small stones. The Apache on the left popped up, and Chance was waiting for him. At the first hint of movement, he squeezed. The warrior straightened as the bullet slammed into him, his arms flailed for a second, and he was gone.

But it was just beginning.

23

AT LONG RANGE, they exchanged sporadic gunfire for nearly an hour. After Chance had killed the first Apache, neither side had been able to tip the balance. Lone Wolf had fallen back, and the three men formed a rough line, more or less parallel to the canyon, but more than a hundred yards distant from it.

Chance knew they had to break the stalemate, but how? A frontal assault was suicide. The warriors had a tailor-made rampart. They could move laterally, though not easily, and when they did expose themselves to fire, it was for fractions of a second at most, just long enough to aim and fire. Then they would drop down to jerk another shell into the chamber.

But if they could be outflanked, there might be a chance to smoke them out. Chance darted out from

behind his rock and raced to Lone Wolf's little bar-
ricade. He dove to the ground as two warriors took
turns firing at him. Lone Wolf and Juanito returned
fire, giving Chance the margin he needed.

Lying there on the ground, he took several seconds to regain his breath and his composure.
When he could talk, he quickly outlined his plan.
It would require speed, and more than a little risk,
but anything was better than this war of attrition
they were waging.

Lone Wolf seemed skeptical, but agreed to go
along. At Chance's signal, his allies started firing
and Chance got to his feet and raced far to the
right. He used what little cover there was for his
broken sprint, ducking from bush to boulder to
scrub. When he stopped running, he was outside
the right wing of the Apache line.

There wasn't much cover for him, but there was
a bit, and it would just have to be enough. He
raised his hand and Lone Wolf sprinted to the left.
They were stringing out their line of defense, leaving the defector vulnerable to a headlong assault
up the middle, but it was the only way.

Lone Wolf was ready. He raised a hand, and
Chance darted forward. Lone Wolf and the defector concentrated their fire on the right flank. The
last Apache in line tried repeatedly to get a shot
off, but as soon as he moved, somebody fired at
him.

Chance sprinted for a point about fifty yards to the Apache's left, putting him outside the line. He hit the ground, skidded to a halt scant inches from the canyon rim. He brought his carbine to bear, waiting to see what would happen. He knew where the closest Apache was. The others were far enough away that they would need a perfect shot to hit him. With the nearest warrior pinned down, he was relatively safe.

Chance rolled parallel to the rimrock. Now it was Lone Wolf's turn. Chance raised his arm high overhead. He saw the scout break for the canyon. Laying down a covering fire, he and the defector kept the warriors pinned. Twice, warriors popped up only to drop out of sight as bullets clawed the earth within inches. Chance was in almost perfect position. His line of sight ran straight along the canyon. He could see all four of the Apache positions without moving his head. Covering them all was a simple matter of shifting the Winchester by a couple of inches.

Lone Wolf reached his position on the rim. Now they had a man on either end of the Apache line. The defector could stay where he was, a threat to any warrior who tried to climb up and over the edge. The scout raised his hand and Chance slipped over the lip of the rock and dropped to the ground more than a dozen feet below. His feet clad only in moccasins, he landed silently. Now all he had to do was work his way toward Lone Wolf, who would be working back toward him. They could squeeze the line, or take the Apaches out one by one.

It was a beautiful plan.

If it worked.

And if it didn't, it wouldn't much matter.

The going was rough. Chance had to pick his way through winding, maze-like channels among the boulders, sometimes turning a corner and staring at a blank wall, other times making ten yards of progress only to find himself in a cul-de-sac and having to double back.

He heard gunfire at the other end of the line. Three shots, then another. Then silence.

Crawling up the face of a flat wedge of red sandstone, he tried to gauge his distance. As near as he could tell, he had covered half the distance between himself and the first Apache. But the Indian was almost certainly moving. At the top of the slab, he was dead even with the canyon rim.

Peeking over the edge of the slab, he waited for some sign of movement. There was none.

Chance crawled up and over, then slid on his haunches a good fifteen feet down a smooth rock face, tilted at nearly forty-five degrees. He hit bottom with a shock that made his teeth ache. Every bone in his body seemed in combat with its neighbors on either side.

He flexed his sore knees, found they worked, and sprinted ten yards to the next cover. He started to peer around a rounded boulder, stopped for some reason he wasn't sure of, and waited.

Had he heard something, he wondered. Or was it nerves?

Listening intently, he held his breath waiting for the least sound, grains of sand grinding together under a moccasin, buckskin scraping against stone. Even a sharp intake of breath.

Nothing.

Chance tried to climb up the boulder, but it was too tall for him to reach its top, and the face of the huge stone offered no handholds. Backing up several paces, he darted forward, launched himself in the air and just managed to catch the top edge. It was flat and nearly smooth, but he dug in his nails and fingertips, pressing his body against the rock to use friction where possible. Scraping the soles of his moccasins against the stone, he tried to lever his body up far enough to get his elbows over the edge.

Twice he rapped his right elbow and lost his grip. The skin was scraped away, and he felt the fire of raw flesh exposed to the air. On the third try, he managed to get his left arm flat on the boulder and used his legs against the sheer face of rock against the boulder's left side to push him up and over.

A bullet slammed into the wall right beside his head, the crack of the impact making his ears ring. Chance tried to melt into the stone. He didn't know where the shot came from.

He rolled to his left and tumbled off the far side of the boulder. He landed heavily on his side. The air was knocked from his lungs, and he doubled over in pain as an Apache rounded another rock not ten yards away. Chance rolled, reaching for his Colt at the same instant. The Apache charged him and Chance fired twice.

Both bullets struck the warrior in the chest. He stopped, his eyes crossed and tried to look down, as if they wanted to see what hurt so much. He staggered now, and sat down, his palms pressed flat against his chest.

Chance fired a third time and the Apache fell over. Chance tried to get up, but he couldn't breath. His chest felt as if it were full of fire. He gasped for air, his voice choking in his throat as he moaned with the pain.

A second Apache appeared around the corner and Chance fired again, this time missing.

He was trapped in the open, and couldn't run because he couldn't get up, let alone run. A shadow fell over the top of the stone behind which the Apache had ducked and Chance looked up, moving only his eyes. Juanito stood there ready to launch himself. The warrior must have sensed something because he darted out at the same instant, his eyes looking for the source of the shadow instead of at Chance.

Juanito hurled himself at the same instant Chance fired at the warrior. The shot missed, and Juanito caught the warrior with one arm as he flew past. The impact staggered the warrior. Juanito landed hard as the warrior stumbled a couple of steps and spun around. Chance fired again, missed and the warrior fired his own gun. He shot Juanito in the head, then turned toward Chance. He fired his last bullet. His breath was coming back, but not enough for him to get up.

The Apache groaned as a bright red blotch appeared on his right shoulder. He tried to work the lever on his Winchester, but couldn't do it one-handed. He flipped the rifle in the air, caught it by the barrel and raised it high over his head. He staggered toward Chance, the rifle moving in tiny circles in the air.

Chance tried to crawl, but he had no strength. There was a sudden rush of footsteps and Chance closed his eyes, certain it was all over. He heard a groan and opened his eyes again to see Lone Wolf, a bloody knife in his hand. The warrior had dropped the club, and clutched at his throat, which gaped like an open mouth, then he dropped straight down, as if his legs had dissolved beneath him.

Chance noticed the blood on Lone Wolf's shoulder. At first, he didn't realize the scout had been wounded. He was groggy, not seeing clearly and barely able to think. He lay there gasping as Lone Wolf sank down beside him.

"Juh's gone," he said. Lone Wolf swallowed hard, looked at the two dead warriors and closed his eyes. Slowly, Chance recovered himself. It still hurt to breathe, but at least he could manage shallow gasps.

When he could speak, he asked, "Where?"

Lone Wolf shook his head. "To meet Wiley, maybe. Maybe to Mexico."

"We have to get him."

Lone Wolf smiled a thin smile. "You have to get him," he said. "I will come after you, but you have to go ahead. If you wait for me, Juh will meet Wiley and make his escape. Wiley will go back to Alamosa. Then he will belong to the army, not to you. You have to get him now."

Chance managed to sit up. His vision was sharper now, and he looked at Lone Wolf's shirt. It was soaked with blood all down the right side. The wound was a bad one.

"Go now," the scout said.

"We have to get you fixed up, first."

"No time."

"There's time. I have the rest of my life."

He crawled to the Apache's side and unbuttoned

the bloody shirt. He worked quickly, fashioning a compression bandage from the shirt of one of the dead warriors.

The wound was worse than he thought, and Lone Wolf had already lost a lot of blood. When he was finished, he started gathering ammunition from the dead Apaches.

Chance draped several belts of Winchester ammunition over one shoulder, as well as one fully loaded gunbelt of shells for the Colt. He stood over Lone Wolf.

"Can you walk?" he asked.

The Apache nodded. He tried to get up, but it was obviously painful for him.

Lone Wolf sat down again. "You go," he said. "I will come later. Blue Mesa. Juh might be wounded. I think I hit him, but I am not sure."

"I'll find him."

Lone Wolf nodded, and closed his eyes again.

24

IT WASN'T HARD to follow the Apache. Lone Wolf had been right, Juh was wounded. With the field glasses, Chance was able to spot him, riding hard but not flat out. Too weak to keep control of his horse, Chance guessed. Leaning over in the saddle, one arm flapping at his side like the broken wing of a bird.

Beyond him, Blue Mesa sprang up out of the ground, appearing to float above it. The huge block of stone seemed to hang in the air, and if he didn't know it couldn't, he couldn't tell, even with the binoculars. The huge block of reddish blue sandstone just seemed to be there, in the middle of nowhere. Chance wondered where it had come from. Was it something left behind after everything round it had been scraped away? Or was it something that grew where nothing had been before?

And out there somewhere, he knew, was Tucker Wiley. If Chance was careful, Juh would lead him right to the bastard. Trailing across the flat desert was no problem, even for Chance. Lone Wolf had taught him something, but there was no substitute for the naked eye. As long as he kept the wounded warrior in sight, he had a chance.

And a chance was all he wanted. Just one. The chance to look into Wiley's eyes and ask him one single question—why? He couldn't imagine the answer, couldn't imagine that there even was one. But he had to ask. He honestly wanted to know. The last few days, the swath of carnage a mile wide carved out of the wilderness seemed so pointless. But it couldn't be. There had to be an explanation, maybe one that only Tucker Wiley knew. But before the sun went down, Chance would have it.

And then he would kill Wiley.

He knew the army was behind him, but not how far. Twice he had stopped to use the glasses on his tail, but hadn't seen so much as a smudge of dust to the north to indicate the approach of an army unit. As far as he could tell, he was alone in the desert with a wounded Apache and the man who had called this outrage down upon them all.

For money, if Lone Wolf was right. Crook had admitted as much. But money, no amount of it, could not justify the things that had happened in the last few days. Chance didn't even know how many people were dead. If one was too many, how many was enough? But in his gut he knew the answer to that question.

Two more.

And then he saw it. A tiny spot creeping toward Blue Mesa, far off to the left. It looked like a bug, crawling out of the haze. He thought of a story he had read once, by Edgar Allan Poe, about a bug that crawled down a shade pull, and how the man watching it had been terrified, not knowing how tiny it was. And Chance was frightened that he had made the opposite mistake.

This seemed so tiny, this crawling thing, like a gnat on a buffalo, but it had to be more than that. There had to be something more than he knew or understood. Maybe the thing he saw was huge, and he didn't realize it. Maybe it would just keep on rolling toward him, getting larger and larger until it dwarfed him then ran him down, grinding him into the barren earth and leaving behind a smear of bloody pulp on the ground.

Maybe he couldn't get even after all, because he was nothing. He was a nobody with a grudge. Chance tried to brush the thought aside. "You're thinking too much," he whispered. "Let it be. Just do what you have to."

He was gaining on Juh, but the Apache was still way out ahead of him. The Indian had changed course now, heading toward the left-hand corner of the mesa. He must have spotted the little smear in the haze, too. And Chance knew, without even having to think about it, that the smear was one of Tucker Wiley's wagons. Probably full of ammunition for a dozen dead Indians. Only Juh remained alive. But Wiley couldn't know that. He wouldn't turn back. He would keep on until Juh met him and told him what had happened.

But by then it would be too late. Chance would be close enough to do what he had to do.

As if by instinct, he let his hand drop to the butt of the Winchester, to rest on the scarred wood. Four miles, that's all that stood between him and the only thing that mattered anymore. Four miles—twenty one thousand feet.

He threw the glasses on the crawling smudge again. It was a wagon, there could be no doubt. Two men sat on the seat, a third rode alongside. One of them had to be Tucker Wiley, but which?

And as he rode, he debated whether to take Wiley first or last. First seemed prudent. That way, he would make sure. But last seemed more fitting, almost biblical in its symmetry. But which man was he?

Shifting the glasses slightly, he caught Juh in the tilted figure-eight of the binocular field. The Apache was having trouble staying on his mount. Leaning forward, one arm circled around the stallion's neck, he seemed to be hanging on by sheer willpower. But that was alright, because there was a place for him, too, in that symmetry.

At three miles, he was no more than a thousand yards behind the wounded Apache. He was certain the wagon crew would see him, but he didn't care. Chance leaned over and pulled his carbine, carrying it in his left hand and controlling his mount with his right. For a moment, he thought about stopping, waiting to see what would happen, but he didn't want to take the chance that he might lose them.

The wagon veered to its left now, heading toward the foot of the mesa. A plume of dust curled up behind it and as it changed course, the dust slowly drifted into a cloud, obscuring the wagon. The Apache changed course and angled his mount toward the towering blue wall of stone. Chance had halved the distance between him and Juh and prodded his horse to go even faster.

Two miles.

The closer he got to the mesa the more overpowering it became. It was the only thing for miles taller than a saguaro, its smooth, almost featureless face growing craggy and scarred as the shimmering haze began to thin. He could see scrubs and mesquite, cactus and even what looked like a joshua clinging to the sheer face.

The wagon had stopped now, not fifty yards from the base of the mesa. The Apache covered the last mile with a renewed burst of energy, sitting up-right in the saddle. Juh wobbled a bit, but hung on. Chance saw the Apache dismount, stumble and fall to one knee. The three-man wagon team ran to meet him, helped him to his feet and pulled him toward the wagon.

Chance skidded to a halt not two hundred yards away. He was out of rifle range. The men at the wagon took cover behind it and fired a ragged vol-ley, but the bullets missed him by several feet.

A lucky shot might nail him, so he dropped to a crouch, but kept on coming, zig-zagging across the hot sand. At a hundred yards, he got down on one knee. The men fired another volley, this time com-ing closer, and Chance pitched forward. There was nothing between him and the wagon but ripples in the desert floor and stunted clumps of cactus. Twenty yards ahead, he could see the edge of a dry wash and he scrambled toward it on hands and knees, nearly losing his Winchester in the process. He tumbled in and lay there panting while he plot-ted his next move.

When he had recovered his wind, he poked his head up then pulled it back. Two bullets chipped the edge of the wash, and sent a cascade of dry sand down over his head and shoulders.

Crawling to the right, he moved about twenty yards, levered a shell home, and counted to ten. He tried to visualize the wagon, knowing he'd have only a split second of surprise until one of the men spotted him. He could aim and fire in that split second, then he'd have to move. He wanted to get it right the first time. Even wounded, Juh was a threat, and the white men had him three to one.

When he was ready, he popped up, sighted and squeezed, all in one motion. He was already on the way down by the time the shock slammed into his shoulder.

This time, he moved only five feet, back in the direction he'd come. Peeking cautiously over the edge of the wash, he thought he saw a man prostrate on the ground, but he wasn't sure. He ducked down again and heard the crack of the rifle an instant later then, a few seconds behind it, the distant slap of the echo bouncing off the blue rock.

This time, he stayed where he was. Instead of popping up, he moved slowly, barely raising his head above the edge. With his eyes right at ground level, he could make out the location of two of the men. The third was nowhere to be seen. And Juh was out of sight.

He slipped the Winchester up, drew a bead, and sent a slug into the body of the wagon, jerked another one in and fired again. This time, he got lucky. A bright red fountain spurted from just above a bent knee. He ducked down again, then realized where Juh had gone. The Apache was almost to the edge of the wash, far to the left. If he made it, Chance would have to go to meet him on hands and knees because the wash was too shallow for him to stand upright without exposing himself to fire from the wagon.

He drew a quick bead and fired, narrowly missing the Apache, who was nearly a hundred and fifty yards away. The Apache kept moving, grabbing at the earth with both hands and literally pulling himself across the ground. Chance popped up a second time, aimed, and fired again.

He saw the Apache curve his spine like a trout trying to throw off a hook. His legs twitched, and then he lay still. Chance smiled, a slight flicker of his compressed lips, brief as summer lightning.

But where was Wiley?

Chance lay there, his head just below the edge of the wash and tried to decide what to do.

Almost unconsciously, he became aware of a vibration in his throat. Without thinking, he had started shouting. Only then did the words register.

"Wiley . . . give it up."

The words, garbled by distance and smashing against the stone, came back an unintelligible bellow.

"Wiley . . . eee . . . eee. Give it up . . . pp . . . pp!"

Peering out again, he saw two figures above the wagon. It didn't register immediately what it meant. When it did, he scrambled up. Two men were climbing up the mesa. Chance charged the wagon.

He could see the wounded white man curled in a ball behind a wheel. When Chance reached him, he made no move, just lay there moaning, his hands folded over his bleeding leg.

"Which one's Wiley?" Chance asked.

The man ignored him.

Chance drew his Colt. He knelt beside the bleeding man. Poking him under the chin with the barrel of the .45, he said, "One more time. Which one's Wiley?"

The man shook his head.

"I'll kill you now." He cocked the Colt.

"Wait."

"I don't have time to wait."

"Alright, alright. The green shirt . . ." Chance reached down, took the man's pistol and hurled it as far as he could. It arced through the air, catching the sun and sparkling like a shiny pinwheel until it shattered against the stone at the foot of the mesa.

The two men were already a quarter of the way up. Chance broke into a run. He found a narrow trail, scrapes in the dirt left by bootheels marring its dry as bone surface. He looked up. Aiming the Winchester carefully, he waited. A hat appeared, and he waited a little longer. A checkered shirt. Not Wiley.

He squeezed.

The blue shirt suddenly peeled away from the

rock wall. Chance watched the awkward swandive until the body hit bottom. Now there was only Wiley.

Chance started up the winding trail, working his way carefully through jumbled stone, skirting the narrow edge and watching the trail ahead of him. Once, he saw a flash of green among the dark bluish-red stone. But it came and went so quickly, he didn't get off a shot.

The hatred in him was gone. He felt nothing now. His mind was concentrated on a single purpose, and passion had no part in it. There was nothing inside him but the determination to finish it. At one hundred feet, he looked out over the valley floor. Far to the north, he saw the dust cloud. He knew what it was.

And still Wiley kept climbing. Chance called to him once, but his voice floated out away from the rock and died unanswered. Columns and flutes of stone jutted up out of the ground, sometimes forcing him to squeeze between them and the sheer face of the mesa, sometimes making him skirt their outer edges on tiptoe.

He could see the rim now, fifty feet above him. As he looked up, the stone wall seemed to tilt toward him. His head swam with the giddy sensation that the entire mesa was about to topple over, pinning him beneath it. He closed his eyes for a moment, waiting for his equilibrium to return.

And at thirty feet, Wiley suddenly appeared, seventy yards down the rim. The man scrambled toward the top in a final burst of energy and hauled himself up and over. Chance fired once, but his precarious footing didn't permit a careful aim. The bullet threw sparks a foot from Wiley's hip, and then he was gone.

The odds had suddenly shifted again. But Chance wasn't going back.

Chance scrambled toward the top. The carbine was hampering him, and he left it behind. Just below the rim, he drew the Apache's pistol from his belt. He had to jump to catch the rim and started to haul himself up. He threw his right leg up and over. Footsteps rushed toward him. A pistol shot cracked, and he felt a stabbing pain in his thigh.

The Colt slipped from his hand and fell over the edge. Ignoring the pain, he rolled to the right, once, then twice. Another pistol shot, this one narrowly missing him. He sat up as Wiley charged.

Thirty feet away, Wiley pulled the trigger again. The hammer clicked.

The gun was empty.

Wiley stopped.

Chance nodded. Wiley started to back up as Chance climbed to his feet. His leg would barely take his weight. Wiley started to run, fumbling with his gun, trying to reload. Chance fired. The bullet slammed into the dirt at Wiley's heels.

Twenty-five yards away, Wiley turned, locking the reloaded pistol. Chance felt no urgency now, just a pervasive calm. He limped toward Wiley, who raised his gun and fired once, then again. But Wiley was nervous. The shots went wide. Chance aimed carefully.

"Why?" he asked.

Wiley stared back without a word.

"Why?" Chance asked again.

Again Wiley said nothing. His silence was the only answer. He was a cipher, a zero. Incomprehensible as stone, and just as mute. And because of him, Jenny was dead. Dalton Junior and Curt were dead. Probably Lone Wolf. And how many others? He cocked his Colt.

And Chance pulled the trigger.

Now Available from HarperTorch,
Classic Westerns
from the *New York Times* bestselling author

Elmore Leonard

←——————→

VALDEZ IS COMING
0-380-82223-7/$5.99 US/$7.99 Can

HOMBRE
0-380-82224-5/$5.99 US/$7.99 Can

THE BOUNTY HUNTERS
0-380-82225-3/$5.99 US/$7.99 Can

ESCAPE FROM FIVE SHADOWS
0-06-001348-6/$5.99 US/$7.99 Can

THE LAW AT RANDADO
0-06-001349-4/$5.99 US/$7.99 Can

GUNSIGHTS
0-06-001350-8/$5.99 US/$7.99 Can

FORTY LASHES LESS ONE
0-380-82233-4/$5.99 US/$7.99 Can

Also Available by Elmore Leonard

PAGAN BABIES
0-06-000877-6/$7.99 US/$10.99 Can

TISHOMINGO BLUES
0-06-000872-5/$25.95 US/$39.50 Can

Available wherever books are sold or please call 1-800-331-3761
to order.

ELW 0902